"I can be a jerk—just ask around—but not tonight."

AJ's words drifted over Pepper's head, making her hair move.

She relaxed into his embrace, surrounded not only by his warmth but by something more. A comfort that surprised her because she wanted to lean into him, let him take on her fear, disappointment and anger. Just for ten seconds. Yes, for ten seconds, she could let someone else take on the responsibility. She wrapped her arms around him, pressing her face into his shoulder, into the muscled solidity of him. Substantial and safe.

She counted off the seconds in her head, but somewhere around six, her brain stopped and she let herself just *feel*. He pulled her more tightly against him. She wanted to melt into him.

"Pepper?"

She looked up at him. His gaze roamed over her face, and she felt herself soften and heat. She tipped up her chin, offering herself to him.

No. She couldn't. She needed to step away. She needed to—

Dear Reader,

Kentucky and cowboy don't go together like peanut butter and jelly...or do they? I watched the television series *Justified*, featuring a Kentucky lawman in cowboy hat and boots. That kernel of an idea led to my next story in the Angel Crossing, Arizona series.

AJ McCreary, my Bluegrass State cowboy (who isn't a lawman), has had a rough few months, finding out he has a daughter and her mama wants cash in exchange for custody. Then his mentor and friend dies. AJ quits bull riding to care for his baby girl and heads west to look for work and pay his respects at his friend's memorial. That's when things get really interesting. He meets his mentor's stepdaughter, Pepper Bourne, a practical and caring physician's assistant who is committed to keeping Angel Crossing healthy and whole. With a cast of characters both human and animal, these two find themselves at odds and in love.

As I write new stories, I don't forget about my other characters, bringing them back for guest appearances. I love being able to see what they are up to and how life is treating them. Next in Angel Crossing, the retired bull rider/mayor and baby brother of the Leigh sisters meets up with his first love and rides again.

If you want to know more about my inspirations and musings or drop me a note, check out my website and blog at heidihormel.net, where you can also sign up for my newsletter. Or connect with me at Facebook.com/authorheidihormel, Twitter.com/heidihormel and Pinterest.com/hhormel.

Yee-haw,

Heidi Hormel

THE KENTUCKY COWBOY'S BABY

——

HEIDI HORMEL

Recycling programs
for this product may
not exist in your area.

ISBN-13: 978-0-373-75724-4

The Kentucky Cowboy's Baby

Copyright © 2016 by Heidi Hormel

Printed in U.S.A.

With stints as an innkeeper and radio talk show host, **Heidi Hormel** settled into her true calling as a writer by spending years as a reporter (covering the story of the rampaging elephants Debbie and Tina) and as a PR flunky (staying calm in the face of Cookiegate). Now she is happiest penning romances with a wink and a wiggle.

A small-town girl from the Snack Food Capital of the World, Heidi has trotted over a good portion of the globe, from Tombstone in Arizona to Loch Ness in Scotland to the depths of Death Valley. She draws on all of these experiences for her books, but especially her annual visits to the Grand Canyon State for her Angel Crossing, Arizona series.

Heidi is on the web at heidihormel.net, as well as socially out there at Facebook.com/authorheidihormel, Twitter.com/heidihormel and Pinterest.com/hhormel.

Books by Heidi Hormel

Harlequin American Romance

The Surgeon and the Cowgirl
The Convenient Cowboy
The Accidental Cowboy

Thanks to my editors, who don't say no when I suggest llamas, alpacas or cowgirls and cowboys who don't fit the mold.

Chapter One

EllaJayne was gone. The car seat in the back of the battered king-cab pickup was empty, the door hanging open. Even flat-as-a-pancake Oggie, her toy doggie, had vanished. AJ had been right there, fixing the loose hose while his daughter slept in her safest-for-its-price-tag car seat. He'd been standing *right there*. He hadn't heard a damned thing. He should have a loyal dog so no one could sneak up and— *Call the cops*, his mind snapped.

He pulled out his phone as he scanned the dusty lot stretching behind a stuccoed cement-block building. Empty, except for a purple SUV. He ran, his well-worn boots kicking up whirls of bleached-out grit. No EllaJayne in or behind the small SUV. How could he have forgotten she was Houdini in a diaper? No sign of her in the dirt-and-gravel parking lot baking in the Arizona high-noon sun. The emergency operator picked up as he raced back to his grimy truck for one more check in every nook, cranny and crevice.

"What's your emergency?" the operator asked.

"My daughter's gone." He ran for the short alley that ran along the building and onto the main street. "Shit," he said.

"Excuse me, sir?"

He kept moving. "Get the police out here. She might have gone onto the road."

"I'll need your location, please."

Her voice was too calm. He wanted to reach through the phone and tell her that his baby girl had disappeared. Instead, as he panted for breath against the heat and the pain in his hip, he said, "I'm in Angel Crossing. I only stopped for a minute to check the truck before I went to find Gene's—" He stopped the rush of words. None of that mattered. "My daughter is sixteen months old. She has dark hair and eyes."

"What's she wearing, sir?"

"Purple shirt with sparkles."

"A little more information, then the police will contact you. I'll need your full name, place of—"

He hung up. He couldn't run and talk. They should be sending police, the K-9 unit, not asking him stupid questions. He stared up and down the uneven, broken sidewalk that stretched in front of the bright-colored facades of empty buildings. Had someone driven in and stolen his daughter while he'd had his head under the hood? A wailing, escalating cry drifted to him. He squinted without his hat brim to shade his McCreary-gray eyes, hoping to catch a glimpse of his sturdy toddler daughter, with hair as dark as his own, its straight-as-a-preacher silkiness direct from her out-of-the-picture mama. He took off, ignoring the sharp bite of pain in his hip and back.

Was the crying closer? The familiar piercing sob was one he'd come to dread, his daughter letting him know he had no business calling himself her daddy.

"EllaJayne. Where are you, baby?" He kept moving as he yelled, not caring that his Kentucky twang had thickened. The cries stopped. He stopped. Where the hell was she? Dear Lord, he'd been so sure he was better than any foster parent or her mama could be. Now he'd lost his baby girl.

After searching another five minutes without hearing her voice again, AJ turned back the way he'd come, moving as fast as he could down the uneven concrete. Where the heck was she? He stepped into a hole where there should have been sidewalk and sharp pain shot down his leg. He hobbled two more steps until the sign for the police department and town hall sprang up like an oasis in the desert. He raced toward it and yanked open the door into a narrow lobby with plastic signs lining the walls. He scanned them looking for…on the right, a small sign in red declared: POLICE. He hurried to the door. Beyond it, a battered metal desk with neat in and out trays stood empty. He didn't hear anything.

"I want to report a missing child." He raised his voice, needing to talk with someone, right now, or he'd—

"What the hell's going on?" asked a tall, blond, unexpectedly familiar man. "AJ? What are you doing here?"

"My daughter." He pulled in as deep a breath as he could with his heart pounding enough to hurt his ribs. "Are you a cop now? I need a search party."

"Not a cop. Mayor. So you're the daddy."

"Where is my daughter?" he asked slowly, with menace. He wasn't playing here. No matter this was Danny Leigh, his old partner in crime. The big blond angel—fitting that he was mayor of a place called

Angel Crossing—to AJ's dark-haired and black-hatted devil.

"Pepper said she found the baby walking around by herself."

"Where is she?"

"I don't mean to tell you your business, but—"

AJ had been right there under the hood while Baby Girl slept after hours of crying. He'd been right there. "I'm getting my daughter." AJ turned from Danny, whom he'd last seen at a rodeo in Tulsa. Now it seemed neither of them was following the money on the back of a bull.

AJ listened for his daughter's cries, but the blood roared so loudly in his ears he wouldn't have been able to hear a jet take off.

"Let me get the chief," Danny said, his hand on AJ's arm. Tight. AJ hadn't lost an ounce of muscle since "retiring." He used it to throw off his friend. Danny let go but stayed beside AJ, saying, "I heard them talking about calling Child Services."

Every one of AJ's straining muscles tightened until his back sent a shooting pain down into his still-aching hip. Even if he'd been able to speak, he wouldn't have known what to say to such crap, except a lot of four-letter words, which he tried not to use anymore because of EllaJayne. Everything he did now was to protect her. He'd quit riding bulls and wrangling for the rodeo.

No one was taking his daughter. He'd rescued her once. He'd do it again. AJ moved past Danny to the doorway beyond the desk. Finally, he heard voices and—"EllaJayne," he shouted, except he felt like he'd been gut-punched and only had enough air for the shout to be a strained whisper.

Danny moved past him in the narrow hallway, through an open archway on the left and said, "She belongs to my buddy. He's one hell of a bull rider."

AJ followed him into the room with a fridge and microwave. There she was. Baby Girl in the arms of a woman wearing scrubs, her hair in a no-nonsense golden-brown ponytail. The disapproving line of the woman's mouth couldn't mar its soft pink charm. He held out his arms for his daughter. EllaJayne lifted her head from the woman's shoulder, tear tracks silvery bright on her rounded cheeks where strands of her McCreary raven-black hair lay in a sticky mess. His heart hurt. His baby girl had been crying…again. He sucked at this father stuff.

"She was wandering around on her own. She could have ended up getting hit by a car or kidnapped," said the woman's voice, firm and soft at the same time.

"My daughter," AJ said as he continued to hold out his now shaking hands. The woman glared at him.

"Absolutely not," she said, clutching the girl tighter to her.

He dropped his arms. "I was fixing a hose. She was asleep."

"You should have been paying more attention," whispered the woman as she patted the little girl's back, soothing her into laying down her head. "I found her wandering and brought her to the police. I could probably report you for neglect. I'm a physician's assistant and we're obligated by law to—"

"Neglect?" AJ didn't try to keep his voice down

and Baby Girl's head popped up. He moved closer to snatch EllaJayne away.

A large man stepped in front of him. Where had this guy come from? "Now, sir, I'm Chief Rudy and we need to have a talk before I can release your daughter to you."

The man, just shy of AJ's six feet two inches with close-cropped, cop-style graying brown hair, took AJ by the shoulder with a big hand and steered him out of the break room and down the hall. He directed him into a cramped office. "Sit." The chief pointed to a chair across from a wooden desk that nearly filled the room, his steel-blue gaze clearly telling AJ he was taking the situation seriously. "Seems like you know our mayor, but I still want details and information so I can check your background." The man pushed a paper across the desk.

AJ felt a yawning chasm of fear and despair opening at his feet. The same one that had been showing up in his nightmares as he and his daughter worked their way across the country, and before that, when he'd learned he had a daughter in foster care. He'd hooked up with her mother during a stint in Kentucky when he'd been drinking more than he should. When he'd first seen EllaJayne… He couldn't think about that now. The police chief wasn't fooling around, no matter this town wasn't much more than a wide place in the road. Then there was the woman, who didn't look old enough to be such a…stick in the mud. Why hadn't she just found him and chewed him out instead of going to the authorities? He focused again on the paper asking for his vital details. He filled it out quickly and handed it to the uniformed chief.

"Stay here while I run this."

AJ stood and paced in what space there was in the room. What the hell would he do if they didn't give him back his daughter? He didn't have money for an attorney. Nothing like this had been covered on any of the parenting sites he'd been reading every night. Other parents didn't lose their kids.

He'd had to fix the truck and she'd been sleeping after screaming at the top of her tiny lungs on their trip into Angel Crossing. He'd only stopped here to pay his respects at Gene's memorial, then they'd head to California, where an old rodeo buddy had promised him work and regular hours. He wasn't going back to Kentucky no matter what.

When he'd found out about EllaJayne less than three months ago, he'd vowed he'd be a better father than any of the long line of McCreary men had been. He'd ditched life on the road and promised himself no women who would come into and out of the little girl's life. She'd already had more knocks than any child deserved.

"Mr. McCreary," the police chief said. "Your record looks clean, other than two drunk and disorderlies. Mayor Leigh said those were 'misunderstandings.'"

AJ relaxed by a millimeter. "I'll take my daughter and be on my way."

"Before you do that, I'd like you to talk with Miss Pepper. I know a little one can be tough to keep track of—you're not the first daddy I've had in here. But… Miss Pepper's heart and her worries are in the right place. Plus, being a medical professional, she's got to be extra careful about these kinds of situations."

AJ stayed silent, following the chief back to the

break room. The Pepper woman was seated at a table, holding his daughter. EllaJayne didn't even turn to him when he said her name. That hurt.

"The little darling's daddy checks out. He's here to take her back." The officer hovered just behind AJ.

"Did you hear that? Daddy's here," Pepper said, turning her head, pinning AJ with a glare of condemnation from her autumn-brown eyes.

"Baby Girl," he said, walking to the woman, holding out his hands for his daughter. Contrary as any McCreary, she pulled away and buried her face in the stranger's shoulder.

PEPPER BOURNE HELD tight to the little girl. No matter what this tall man with his worn jeans and boots said now, he couldn't be much of a father if he hadn't even known his child had wandered off. She'd seen plenty of cowboys like him over the years, especially friends of Daddy Gene's. Just thinking that name still hurt. She snuggled the toddler closer.

"Hand her over," said Chief Rudy. "Kids wander off. It's happened to every parent."

"Are you sure? Her diaper was dirty."

"That happens to all kids, too," the cowboy said swiftly. "I was right there. Under the hood."

"And that worked so well, didn't it? She didn't even have a hat or shoes. What are you doing in town?" Not that it was really her business.

"Come to pay my respects to Gene Daniels. Got word he'd passed, and there was a memorial."

Pepper squeezed the little girl who squeaked in protest. Daddy Gene had been gone for a month. Tears filled her eyes and she couldn't choke out the words. A tiny hand patted her cheek. Pepper feared she would burst into ugly sobs.

"How did you know him?" she asked to distract herself.

"Barely kissin' cousins and the rodeo," the man answered. "Now, if I can have my daughter, I'll be going."

"Chief, I don't know that I'm comfortable with the situation." She stared hard at the toddler's daddy, while ignoring the muscled strength and length of him. "Where's your wife? Your daughter's mother."

"None of that's your business, lady. The police chief here says I'm good to go," he snapped back, his storm-cloud-gray eyes locked on hers.

"That may be but as a health care professional, I have a duty to ensure that any child is not being abused or neglected." She made sure her tone let this cowboy know that he wasn't fit to care for a chicken, let alone a precious little human being.

"Mama," the toddler whimpered and rubbed her forehead into the crook of Pepper's neck.

"Chief, you've got to let me examine her. Who knows how long she was in the sun?"

"Fine. Come on, Mr. McCreary, let's get this settled," Rudy said.

Pepper hesitated for a second. McCreary. That last name struck a chord. She needed to focus on the little girl. Her daddy didn't look like a bad guy. He had dark hair like his daughter's, though his had an unruly curl around his nape and ears. But the little girl hadn't gotten her mink-brown eyes from him. He didn't look or act like an abuser. An outlaw, maybe, a bad-boy rodeo cowboy. Still, it was her duty to make sure the toddler was being cared for properly. She had to give the girl a good once-over.

Followed by the chief and the cowboy holding his daughter's stuffed animal, Pepper carried EllaJayne on her hip, coming out of the building that housed the town hall, the police station, a real estate office, and a law office. The clinic was half a block down on the right, across from the Angel Crossing Emporium of Wonders. The sign, with its painted roadrunner and mountain lion, always made her smile, even though the emporium had closed long ago. The mayor was trying to get a grant to hire artists to paint the plywood and "refresh" the sign to make the town look less abandoned.

The facades along the main road, which was picturesquely called Miners Gulch, had been added in the 1970s to entice tourists to the town, as the nearby mine and the county's biggest employer started to close its operations. Tourists hadn't been lured in, but the townsfolk had come to love the signs that gave the vibe of a Spaghetti Western set. Or a bona fide ghost town. The problem was a ghost town was a dead town. With no good jobs, Angel Crossing was edging toward that as the younger residents scattered to the wind. Pepper was the exception, rather than the rule. Although technically, she wasn't local, not having moved to town until she was seven.

Today wasn't the day to worry about Angel Crossing. She had a little darling in her arms who needed her attention. Like the old-timey facades, her clinic had the feeling of a bygone era. It served residents well enough, even if it housed more than one piece of equipment that should have been in a museum. She did what she could for her patients, many of them retired and living on minuscule pensions and Social Security. She regularly had to beg, borrow and nearly steal supplies, especially free samples. She knew of more than one patient who skimped on medications to pay for food. That's why the garden would make such a difference.

"Oggie," EllaJayne said into Pepper's ear, reaching out with her hand and flexing her fingers. Pepper followed her gesture and saw the girl's cowboy daddy, still holding onto the flattened stuffed animal she'd given him. The man had a hitch in his step that didn't keep her from noticing his rodeo swagger. He needed a hat. What cowboy didn't have a hat? It would have shaded his handsome face. Pepper knew trouble and she didn't need anyone to tell her this guy was that plus more. She also didn't need anyone to tell her that his kind of trouble could give a woman memories to warm up her nights.

Pepper focused on the bundle in her arms as she walked into Angel Crossing Medical Clinic. "I'm going to Exam One," she said to Claudette, her right-hand woman at the reception desk.

"Who is this?" asked Claudette, her short dark hair streaked with highlights and spiked to fit her warrior-woman attitude in a grandmother's body.

"We'll give you everything as soon as I'm done with the exam." The ring of boot heels followed Pepper. An uneven sound. She glanced back and caught the man grimacing. No time to worry about that.

"Okay, little darling, let's just see how your 'daddy' was caring for you." She ignored the snort from the cowboy.

She put him and everything else out of her mind, concentrating on the girl and the exam. She didn't want to miss anything. But other than the dirty diaper— which Pepper changed from her own supplies—and a little diaper rash, the toddler was fine.

"So?" he asked when she finished with the final tug of the girl's T-shirt.

"What about her vaccinations?"

"I… I… Of course she's had them. I have papers in the truck."

He didn't know. "Allergies?"

He stood feet planted and long fingers tapping against his leg. "It's all in her records. She's fine. You just said so."

She'd been working with patients ever since she'd started as an EMT in her teens, and read annoyance in the tightness of his mouth. She also saw fear in the tilt of his head. What to do? The child looked fine.

"You're good to go, then, but little ones are quicker than their parents think and can easily get into things they shouldn't. Let's go see if Claudette can't find cream for the rash." Pepper scooped up the girl and walked out. The exam room as they'd stood there had suddenly gotten smaller. She'd started to think trouble might be what she needed in her life. Because trouble had started to look a lot like a good time, which she hadn't had since…forever. Then smart Pepper reminded not-so-smart Pepper he was a pa- tient's father…and a cowboy. The kind of man she'd long ago figured out wasn't for her. They might look pretty, but the shine wore off quickly.

She kept her gaze on Claudette and glanced at

Chief Rudy, who had an odd look on his face as he stared down at his phone.

"What?" she asked because it was obvious that something had just popped up on the screen.

"I ran his name, but, well, I didn't connect it... Hell—"

This was bad. The chief didn't swear. It was a contest in town to see who could make him curse when they got pulled over or visited the station. The man just didn't get provoked, and if he did, he didn't say bad words. So that meant whatever he'd just discovered was horrible.

"His name is Arthur John McCreary."

"Everybody calls me AJ," the cowboy said irritably.

"You're Daddy Gene's cousin." The words popped out of her mouth in shock as the connection fell into place.

"Yeah, Gene is...was my cousin. I told you that." His voice had thickened with true emotion.

"Welcome to Angel Crossing," Rudy said. "Sorry the circumstances aren't better. Gene was a good man and a good friend."

"Thanks," AJ said and added, "I should have known. How many Peppers could there be in Angel Crossing?" He rubbed his hand over the back of his neck. "Gene talked about you and your mama. Please accept my condolences."

She nodded. Now she remembered him. He rode bulls and had dragged Daddy Gene from the ring when the animals had nearly stomped him to death. The one or two pictures she'd seen of AJ, his black hat had nearly covered his face.

"I guess I should take you to the ranch. Faye would never forgive me if I didn't bring you out to say hello. Daddy Gene hoped you'd come for a visit one day, but I don't think this is how he imagined it."

Chapter Two

Pepper's directions to Gene's ranch had included exact mileages, road names and landmarks. Even in the sameness of the rocky terrain, dotted with gray-green bushes and low trees, he'd easily found the turnoff that wound through a short downhill drive. Flatlands opened up for a distance before moving into another set of foothills that rolled into mountains. The ranch included a low house, outbuildings and corrals. The animals milling around ranged in color from white to shadows-at-noon black. But they weren't cattle or horses or even goats.

He checked his rearview mirror to see his daughter, who was eerily quiet. Her head swiveled back and forth as she looked out the windows, staring wide-eyed, her lost-all-its-stuffing dog clutched tight in her fist.

Contrary as any McCreary, after days on the road wishing she'd quiet down, he wanted noise from his daughter now so he could stop thinking about Pepper. She somehow made scrubs look as good as painted-on jeans and a tight cowgirl shirt. She actually looked better than the buckle bunnies who'd been the honey to his bee for years. EllaJayne's mama had been Miss Kentucky Rodeo two years before he'd met her.

He stopped the truck in front of the house that had a lumpy outline of clearly unplanned additions. It had been Gene's home. He'd talked of the ranch with a lot of pride. Gene had retired from the rodeo circuit after a string of bad wrecks. Both Danny and AJ had tried to talk him out of it because he was the best at reading the animals. They'd been young and hadn't understood what it meant to have a body that had been battered and broken again and again.

AJ knew he couldn't stall any longer. Though he hated to intrude, his nearly maxed-out credit card and flat wallet told him otherwise. He had to swallow that pride and ask—beg for—their hospitality. He'd stay for the memorial, then move on. He'd come west for a brand-new start where no one had heard of the McCrearys of Pinetown, Kentucky.

He held EllaJayne firmly in his arms when he knocked on the weathered door. Up close, the ranch house looked like a cross between a trailer and a cabin.

"There you are," said the woman who opened the door. "Come in." Obviously, this was Faye, just as Gene had described her: "Stevie Nicks who bought her duds at Sheplers and her jewelry at swap meets." She stepped back, pushing a drape of gray-streaked hair with strips of color like her daughter's out of her watchful green eyes.

"Thank you, ma'am," he said, finally remembering the manners that had been knocked into him with a spatula and fly swatter.

"Oh, my," she said as tears filled her eyes. "Don't

you have the look of Gene? It's just like he's here. And those nice manners."

"Yes, ma'am." He and Gene looked nothing alike.

"And who is the gorgeous baby? Yours. Look at that hair, that skin. Oh, my, but she'll be a beauty. Come here, sweetheart," Faye said and held her hands out to his daughter. The little girl went right to her. "I bet I have a cookie you'd like. You can call me Grana. I always wanted someone to call me that. I'm in the Crone phase of my womanhood. The most powerful. You are in the Baby phase, still finding your power. But don't worry. It's there."

He followed her closely in the wake of the deep scent of incense and sharp desert herbs. "Ma'am," he tried, "I'm here to—"

"Have you eaten? No. I can see you haven't. Sit."

"Thank you, ma'am. I know that I should have called as soon as Gene…passed. But I'm here to pay my respects and attend the memorial."

She waved a thin, elegant hand covered in silver and turquoise. "Gene understood. He spoke of you often. Now, I'll fix you a plate and give this little one a cookie."

"Ma'am," AJ interrupted. "I don't want to put you out at a time like this."

"A time like what?"

Jeez. Gene had told him that his wife and he…well, actually not his legally wed wife. They had never married. AJ said gently, "A sad time like this."

"Sad?" She laughed brightly and his daughter joined in. "We're celebrating Gene's life. That can never be sad." Faye walked through a listing doorway into a kitchen filled with brightly painted cabinets and mismatched appliances.

"Now," she went on, "you're a Taurus and you've been traveling, so I think you need scrambled tofu, with sprouted bread, yogurt…no, not yogurt…kefir. Then I'll move in with Pepper so you can have my room."

"Please, I couldn't ask you to do that."

"Of course, you'll stay here. It's what Gene would have wanted."

"I couldn't do that," he protested politely, even though he'd planned to ask for such hospitality.

"I couldn't let Gene's family stay anywhere else." Tears filled her voice and she squeezed EllaJayne closer to her.

AJ couldn't afford to protest too strongly. "If you insist, ma'am."

"Perfect. This food will balance you, and then you'll have a wonderful night's sleep. Here. Hold your daughter while I finish." She plopped the little girl into his arms and magically produced a chunky cookie that EllaJayne immediately started gnawing.

"What's in there?" he asked. This cookie looked like it might have all kinds of things that were bad for babies. Except what were those things? Chocolate? No, that was dogs. What had the website said?

Faye crossed to the stove. "Wheat germ, oats… You ride bulls, Gene said, and you're a Taurus. Isn't it wonderful the way the universe makes things like that work?"

"Used to ride bulls."

"Oh, no, I don't think the universe will like that."

She turned to him and a frown marred her surprisingly smooth brow.

"I don't think the universe is very happy with me right now." EllaJayne looked up at him, the cookie in one hand.

"No," she said clearly. The one word she said regularly and loudly. Her brow wrinkled. *Uh-oh.* He knew that look. That was the look that meant something smelly was going to come out of one end or the other. *Really, Universe, what have I ever done to you?*

PEPPER EXPECTED TO see Daddy Gene come around the side of the house and onto the patio, to greet everyone with a big shout and a laugh, then smooth his handlebar mustache into place before announcing that it was time to get the party started. Except that wouldn't be happening. Faye had tried to make it festive with lights strung around the patio and a table laden with food. Of course, everyone knew the kinds of dishes Faye cooked so a number of pies, casseroles and platters had magically appeared, too.

Pepper saw the mayor chatting with Gene's cousin AJ. The man and his daughter had stayed with them last night at Faye's insistence. Pepper had been so busy between work and getting everything set for the memorial that she'd only been home to sleep. Pepper turned away, not sure exactly what she was feeling. Today was a celebration, she reminded herself, but the weight of responsibility made her shoulders ache. Daddy Gene had been a part of her life since he'd shown up at the commune. Pepper had only been five years old, but she'd known he was the kind of man they both could count on. Now what?

"It's time," Faye announced. "We're here to celebrate the life of my lover, companion and soul mate." Then she started singing "Witchy Woman" while the silence got increasingly uncomfortable.

Dear Lord. Angel Crossing had more or less accepted Faye…they'd loved Daddy Gene and he and Faye were a package deal. Alone, Faye might be just a little too filled with hippie hokum.

Danny stepped up to Faye and stopped her swaying, off-key rendition mercifully short. "That was one of Gene's favorites. You know, he was my mentor… AJ and I wouldn't have stayed on any bull without Gene. He could read those animals like most men read the want ads." Nods rippled through the crowd. Faye smiled at Danny. It might just work out okay. "I'll miss Gene, just like all of us will. But I know he wanted us to have a good time tonight. Drink a little beer—his favorite, Lone Star—jaw a bit and eat good food…and I see the tables are filled. To Gene." Danny lifted his beer bottle and everyone joined in.

Pepper turned away to pull herself together. A celebration, she told herself again. She could do this for Daddy Gene. This one last thing for him. The man who'd been her father and the one person she could count on no matter what. "Love you, Daddy Gene," she said quietly, looking out toward the mountains dark against the brilliant pinks, purples and reds of the sunset. "Thanks for the show." She smiled and then wiped away the tears. Time to honor a life well lived. She wouldn't remember those last days of illness and pain. She'd remember him laughing. That was her favorite Daddy Gene.

"FAYE ASKED ME to do the reading of the will tonight."

Pepper stared at Bobby Ames, Angel Crossing's attorney and part-time taxidermist.

He went on, "Everyone grab a seat. This won't take long."

They were in the living room of the ranch house, sitting on an assortment of chairs salvaged from roadside garbage piles or built by Faye's friends.

"Come along, Pepper Moonbeam," Faye said, formal and stiff. She'd been holding back her sadness tonight so they could "rejoice in" Daddy Gene's life, not mourn his death. Pepper knew how tough that was as she'd worked over and over to hold her own tears in check. He'd been gone for just a month. They'd scattered his ashes weeks ago, but today was the real goodbye and much more painful than the one at his bedside. She didn't understand what the lawyer was doing. Gene had left the ranch to Faye, what else could the will say? My god, he'd named the place for her: Santa Faye Ranch.

Pepper sat and waited for the attorney to speak again, a moment out of a soap opera or a telenovela. Bobby Ames finally started to read the will. Daddy Gene named a couple of friends and gave them his riding gear and two of his trophies. Then Bobby Ames did the strangest thing. He put the will down, sucked in a breath and spoke in a voice that Pepper was sure he'd learned from *Law and Order*. "I want to let you know that if Gene had come to me… I'll just read this, then you can ask questions."

What had Daddy Gene done? Put the rest of the will in verse? Or maybe he'd set up a scavenger hunt for the remaining items, like his bear-claw necklace.

That would be like him. He'd been just a big kid at heart.

"The ranch goes to my cousin and savior, Arthur John McCreary."

Pepper's breath clogged her lungs as she ran over the words again in her head. They didn't make any sense.

"He left me the ranch?" AJ asked. He didn't sound like a man who'd just hit the jackpot.

"You've got the wrong will," Pepper told the attorney. Well, maybe more like accused him of gross incompetence.

"Now…" Chief Rudy started.

"It's wrong," she said. *It's got to be.* She'd used the inheritance she'd been sure she and her mother would get on the grant application to get the Angel Crossing Community Garden Project started. "Daddy Gene always said… I used the property—"

"How could I have forgotten," Faye said with something like regret and worry, two emotions she rarely acknowledged. "You told that agency you would use the value of the ranch as the matching money."

"You did what?" AJ's storm-gray gaze locked on her. No chance that she couldn't figure out what he was thinking. "There's a lien on the property?"

"Not exactly," she said.

He hitched up his sleeping daughter so her head fit more firmly on his shoulder. "You. Me. The attorney. We need to talk now."

"What are you, a caveman? I already told you there's some mistake." She moved closer to whisper what needed to be said so no one—especially not her mother—could hear. "You didn't even visit. When he was…when the doctors said that he…you didn't visit. Why would he leave this to you? Did you call him? Talk to the attorney?"

"Are you saying that I scammed Gene? My God, he was kin. He watched out for me when I first started riding bulls."

"What other reason could there be?"

Bobby Ames pretended to clear his throat.

Pepper moved around the room restlessly as the silence stretched. Not only was her plan on the line, her mother's future was, too. The ranch would have been plenty to keep Faye in yogurt and tofu. One good thing about her mother was that she didn't need a lot of cash to get along. That's why Pepper had been so sure the community garden plan would work.

"Now, we need to discuss this frankly," Bobby Ames said, still using his TV-attorney voice. "There'll be no more talk about this will not being legal. It is. Faye and the chief looked everywhere for another one. There was nothing at the house. I called around to other attorneys and there was nothing. This is his will."

Pepper wanted to say no. She wanted to scream no, but she was nothing if not a realist. She left the dreaming to her mother.

"Why me?" AJ asked.

Yeah, she wanted to know that, too.

Bobby Ames adjusted his glasses. "Could be that it's an old will and you were his cousin? Or maybe because you saved his life."

"I'm not sure I saved him," AJ said, moving his daughter to his other shoulder.

"The way Gene told it was that if you hadn't run into the arena and grabbed him, he'd have been stomped to death. He said the clowns had gotten tangled up with a loose calf and you were the first one to him. He said you took a good kick to the ribs." AJ's hand went to his side. "I believe you nearly lost your spleen."

"He thanked me plenty," AJ said. "I never expected—"

"You don't need to make any decisions today," Bobby Ames said, "except this thing with Pepper and the grant. What did Faye mean?"

Pepper searched for a way to understand the new lay of the land. She'd never imagined Daddy Gene wouldn't leave the ranch to Faye. She'd never asked him about it in those last weeks. They'd all known he was dying but they'd still tried to deny it until the very end.

No one spoke and the silence stretched out long enough that she could hear the deep breathing of the baby. *Come clean, girlie girl,* Daddy Gene's voice said in her head. Dear Lord. What would they do? What would the state office where she'd filed her paperwork say?

Pepper said, "Daddy Gene loved Faye, you all know that. You know what he would do." Her voice squeaked to a stop. Her chest hurt from holding back the tears. She had to get through this next bit, then she could fall to pieces. She needed to protect Faye's future and her own plans for the garden, her patients and the town. Pepper breathed deeply as she'd seen her mother do before a big announcement. "I'm planning the Angel Crossing Community Garden here at the ranch and we needed a grant for the equipment. Faye agreed I could use the value of the ranch's land and outbuildings to match the money the state would grant us. It was the only way to get the money, so I put that on my application. I've already set up the greenhouse using my own savings and promised loans to my farmers. I told you all about it, chief. Remember? There would be fresh food for those who worked the ground and plots where others could grow specialty plants that they'd then sell and pay me land rent. It would be run by a nonprofit and support small businesses as well as senior and children's health. The mayor even agreed it was a good idea."

"It is a good idea," Chief Rudy said, cutting off AJ when he started to protest, "but you didn't tell any of us that you basically were promising money you don't have or that the plan had been put together with a spit and a prayer."

Finally, AJ spoke, his voice low but no less angry. "So you've used my ranch and now there's a lien and I won't be able to sell."

"It seems that you've gone awfully quick from 'I can't believe this is mine' to ordering us all around because you inherited some land," Pepper said, facing him and forcing her voice to be steady. "There isn't a lien on the property. I've only just put in the paperwork. I'm sure I can explain things and rescind the application…if I have to, which I'm not convinced I'll have to."

"It's the Spring Equinox right now," Faye said out of nowhere, as she sometimes did. "This was always Gene's favorite time of year. He said spring was when anything was possible."

Chapter Three

Butch, the Australian shepherd, sat happily in the front seat of Pepper's small SUV. The one her mother had insisted Daddy Gene buy and then paint an eye-searing purple. On the plus side, Pepper was easily recognizable. It meant when she went to homes up in the mountains, her patients immediately recognized her. Faye may have known what she was doing. Maybe. Pepper pushed away the panic and flexed her hands on the steering wheel. "Butch, we're in a lot of trouble, and I don't mean because you sat in Dr. Cortez's chair. I used a ranch I didn't own to try and get money from the government. It's not like they gave me any money or that I lied. I really, really thought the ranch was ours. It was just two weeks after Daddy Gene died. I might not have been at my best, but there was a deadline." The black, brown and white dog with mismatched eyes turned and gave her one of his smiles. Butch had been picked out of a litter of wriggling puppies to herd Faye's Beauties—her alpacas and llamas. She'd talked Daddy Gene into getting the animals about a year ago, about the same time as the ranch that had rented most of Santa Faye Ranch had closed its gates and broken its lease. Faye insisted the fleece from the animals, which she planned to spin and weave, would make up for the lost revenue. Not long after the animals arrived, Daddy Gene had gotten very sick again. Faye had been more worried about him than about making her spinning and weaving venture profitable, even though she loved her Beauties. Butch, who acted like a poodle in a hairy shepherd body, had worked hard with her to earn his good citizen certificate and therapy training. He visited the office on the days it was just her and Claudette. Dr. Cortez, who came to the clinic twice a week, didn't like Butch or believe any animal could help calm patients. Butch actually did a good job with people facing needles—kids and adults alike.

Only two minutes from the ranch, Pepper needed to come up with her talking points fast. She'd avoided AJ and Faye this morning. She had, however, called an attorney—not Bobby Ames—for advice that wasn't free. He'd said she might have a case for overturning the will, and he didn't think she'd end up in jail, probably, for using the ranch to try to get the grant. He'd advised withdrawing the application immediately, but not explaining why unless she was forced to. The goal was to not look like a liar and a cheat to the agency. Pepper understood what he wasn't saying. If she ever wanted Angel Crossing or herself to get another grant from the state or anyone else, she had to clear up this problem quickly and quietly. She'd already started and so far so good.

Pepper parked next to AJ's king-cab pickup, dusty and dented. "Come on, Butch," she said unnecessarily. The dog was already at the front door waiting for her. She gripped her tote tighter and went in.

Butch raced from her side, yipping with excitement. He disappeared into the kitchen. Pepper took papers to review later that night out of her tote, then hung the bag on its hook. She toed off her clogs and slipped her feet into sandals. A place for everything and everything in its place. One of those sayings from kindergarten that had more than a little ring of truth.

Butch ran back to her, his doggy smile stretching across his face. *No more stalling, Pepper.* Butch sprinted ahead of her again. She strained to hear voices.

"Faye, I'm home." That was stupid. Of course she was home. Silence.

Butch trotted into the kitchen and then looked over his shoulder at her. That was his open-the-back-door look. That must be where they were. Pepper sniffed the air. Someone had been cooking. She almost felt sorry for AJ because she knew that smell. Faye had made scrambled tofu, which was okay, but she'd added kimchi, fish sauce and...dear Lord. She smelled the cheese Faye insisted on making—the kind that tasted like dirty socks. Maybe Faye's cooking would convince AJ to move along, except no one would walk away from a ranch.

Butch sat on her foot and leaned against her leg. He really was a remarkable therapy dog. He always knew when anyone was in distress. She patted his warm furry head before making herself a little taller than her five feet seven so she could more easily face the people on the patio. Specifically, the tall, lean AJ.

Faye in Earth Mother mode held EllaJayne as she danced her around the patio. Pepper didn't see AJ, though.

"Faye, where's that child's father? Did you kill him with the kimchi?" Faye's Korean-style sauerkraut had peppers hot enough to singe nose hairs. Pepper didn't eat the kimchi or anything else with peppers—hot or sweet. One of life's little ironies.

"EllaJayne and I are enjoying the rebirth of the world since it's spring. Aren't we? You're an old soul, aren't you, little one?"

"Faye," Pepper said with patience.

"You're thirsty. I can hear it in your voice. Go get a drink." Her mother danced another three steps. "This will all work out for the best."

"Good to know."

"No need for sarcasm, that's the work of a small soul."

"Sorry. It's just that today has been—"

"I know, dear," Faye said, taking the little girl's arm and waving. "There's your daddy."

AJ was a cowboy, from his hip-rolling walk to his well-used boots and frayed-at-the-seams jeans. Pepper couldn't read what he might be thinking. She could guess, though. *Don't borrow from the bank of trouble*, she heard Daddy Gene's voice in her ear. She wanted to snap back at him that she wouldn't need to borrow if he'd just left the ranch to Faye. But he wasn't here. She needed to leave that go.

"You and I need to talk," AJ said in a soft drawling voice that didn't have a hint of friendly.

"Absolutely," Pepper said. Acting confident—even when she wasn't—convinced people that she knew what she was doing. "We can talk in my office."

"No, darling," Faye said. "You should take advantage of the energy of spring and the outdoors." Her mother took the child and walked inside.

"I made some calls," AJ said.

"Okay." She would let him talk so she could figure out what he knew and wanted. She watched him pace around the patio. He definitely was handsome—she had to be honest.

"I spoke with Danny Leigh."

Did he think being the mayor's friend was a big deal? Like she should be impressed? Everybody knew the mayor. This was a small town.

"Telling a state agency you owned land you didn't could end up getting you and the town—including Danny and others who signed the papers—into a lot of trouble."

"Daddy Gene meant for Faye to have the ranch. Everyone in town knew that was his plan." She plowed on, pushing back the tears. "Faye agreed with me about the garden because it would provide food and a chance to earn extra money for anyone who needs help in Angel Crossing. How can you take that from them?"

"This is about what's legal and fair."

"Fair? I'll tell you what's fair. Giving my patients a fighting chance to get healthy with fresh fruits and vegetables. Helping kids understand where what's on their plate comes from and what real food is. What about the entrepreneurs? Liddy already has her name in for a loan to make soaps and salves from the herbs she'll grow. With that money, she can go to the community college, get a degree and earn enough so she can rent a bigger place and be allowed to have her kids back."

"It's the law. The will is clear. The ranch goes to me." He turned his back to her and his shoulders—his wide and muscled shoulders—lifted with a deep breath. "I have plans, too, and they all have to do with giving my little girl the best. Bobby Ames said that it will take months to settle the estate and that's if there are no challenges or issues." He turned and glared at her. "I was going to go to California but it seems that we have a place here. Plus, I need to make sure you don't do anything else with the property that will make it less attractive to a buyer."

She whispered, because that was all the air she had, "You're selling the ranch?"

LOOKING AT PEPPER's horrified face nearly made him take back the truth.

"I can fix this so you don't have to sell. Or—" Her voice trailed off as her shoulders drooped.

He couldn't weaken now. Not only did his future ride on this ranch but his daughter's did, too. For the first time in his life, he had something to lose. "Promises won't put food in me and my daughter's bellies." Good Lord, he heard his daddy in those hard words. He couldn't stop now even if he really believed that he could make this work out for all of them...somehow. "And what will keep me out of trouble if the state doesn't like that you lied on the grant, huh?"

Her gaze dropped. "I've already started withdrawing the application. You don't need to worry."

Good thing for him she'd given in. He'd had about another ten seconds of meanness before he'd have caved. "My original plan had been to stop to pay my respects before heading to California to work on a dude ranch for a buddy of mine. Since the estate might not be settled for months—and it looks like there are a few things to take care of in preparation for a sale and to make sure you don't try anything else with the property—that means EllaJayne and I will need to stay on here, in what's technically my house…or will be. I mean, Bobby Ames explained that until everything is settled, you and Faye don't *have* to let me stay. But hotels get mighty expensive, and there's the attorney to pay, as well as food and diapers and such for EllaJayne. Faye already agreed and you wouldn't put out a little girl. Also, I'll have to look for work, which leads to my next problem. I need someone to look after EllaJayne, from time to time. She likes your mama and since you're a nurse—"

"Physician's assistant," she corrected.

He'd better hurry because she was recovering her spit and vinegar. "Physician's assistant. Danny Leigh vouched for you, too. You and your mama could do in a pinch, but I need to have something steadier, more permanent. So, here's the deal. In addition to staying here, I need your help in tracking down someone to care for my daughter. You've got to know who's good at that sort of thing. Does Angel Crossing have a day care? Either way. I want good care at a reasonable price."

"I'm sure I can give you care recommendations. But I'm a little confused as to why I should be helping *you*? What do I get out of the deal?"

He worked to not admire her backbone. Up against a wall and she wasn't afraid to negotiate. "What's your counteroffer?"

"Since Faye said you can stay, then you should care for Faye's Beauties."

"Her Beauties?"

"The llamas and alpacas. Faye does most of the work but she needs help."

"Seems fair."

Her face had relaxed into a smile. He liked that smile. It shouldn't matter if he liked it or not. His only goal here was getting the ranch free and clear, selling it and moving on. He'd considered staying but he couldn't do that and raise a daughter. Plus he'd never even worked on a ranch. He'd helped with animals at the rodeo but that wasn't the same thing.

"I could write everything up in a contract," he went on, "but I'd like to think we could do this on a shake of the hand?" Despite her hippie mama and using a ranch she didn't own, Pepper was practical and trustworthy, he thought. He'd gotten that impression, anyway, from everything Danny and Bobby Ames had said to him.

Her stiff shoulders and etched-in-stone chin told him she wasn't giving up or giving in without a little more fight. She might have been down, but she wasn't out. "Since you already settled the housing with Faye, I don't see that I can take issue with that. I'm sure I can find your daughter care. She's a sweet baby. I need some assurance you won't sell out from under me *and* I want a chance to buy Santa Faye Ranch before it goes on the market."

"If that's legal, sure, why not." He didn't care who bought the property. He just needed the money. "When everything's settled and I'm ready to sell, I'll let you know."

"Wow. So kind of you to tell me when you plan to sell my home."

He almost laughed at her snarky comment. He might appreciate her backbone and the way she filled out her scrubs… Jeez…what was his problem? "Promise." Her gaze stayed on him. He couldn't look away. "Cross my heart, hope to die, stick a needle in my eye." Now, what had made him say something that juvenile and stupid?

She laughed. "You know, Daddy Gene said that same thing." Suddenly, she stopped smiling.

Her face settled into lines of pain, her eyes darkening. He knew that pain. He was feeling it, too. Missing Gene. The man who'd helped him become…a man, with his rough-and-tumble advice and affection. AJ reached out and dragged her into a hug, pulling her against him to stop the pain, for both of them. "I'm so sorry. I know how much Gene loved you and your mama."

She didn't move and he stared out over her head and into the expanse of scrubby desert and mountains around them. He'd never been in mountains with so little vegetation. In Kentucky, the only time a mountain looked this bad was after mining. Here it was the natural order of things. The lack of green wore on his eyes.

"I miss him. I miss him so much," Pepper said in a hoarse whisper.

AJ wasn't good at this sort of thing, never had been. But he couldn't walk away from her sadness and tears. "I know, honey," he said. He looked down at her, where she'd buried her face into his shoulder. Her hair was pulled back from a center part to a loose and messy bun at the back of her head. It had streaks of golden red in the light brown. The lush fullness surprised him. She appeared so tightly wound except for the softness of her hair, and her brightly colored toenails. No way should he be spending so much time determining the exact color of her hair or noticing that she had daisies painted on her toenails. He relaxed his hold a little, needing some space between them. She clutched at him.

"Not yet," she whispered as a breath shuddered from her.

He brushed his cheek against her temple and he nearly kissed her, wanting to soothe her distress and let her know she wasn't alone. Instead, he held her loosely against him. He could guess what her curves would feel like and what they might do to him if he pulled her closer. He wasn't that much of a dog.

Her scent of spice and citrus filled his head, such a sweet fresh smell. It reminded him of the time between spring and summer, full of promise.

"Did Daddy Gene really talk about us when he was still riding bulls?" she asked, not moving her face from his shoulder.

"Sure." This topic was much safer than where his mind had gone when his hand encountered the sexy deep curve of her waist. He'd just stopped himself from testing the swell of her hip. He kept his eye on a large cactus in the near distance. "He said that Faye loved turquoise and pepitas. Pumpkin seeds." Pepper nodded so he went on. "He said you refused to let him get you another horse when yours died from colic." Crap. Why had he brought up that story? He could feel the sadness course through her as she burrowed into his shoulder again, like she could hide there forever. Surprisingly, he would have let her if it would have helped.

"Toni," she said, her voice muffled. "Her name was Antonia. I didn't think I'd ever not be sad again. For a while, I wanted to be a vet, but then when Daddy Gene got sick the first time, I realized medicine—human medicine—was for me." She relaxed against him.

He wrapped his arms more fully around her, wanting to…he wasn't sure what, other than make her feel better, to lessen the sadness he felt in her every muscle and heard in her voice. She hadn't asked for this any more than he had. They both needed to weather the situation as best they could. He could guess at her sorrow now. It was an echo of his own. He missed Gene. He'd been someone AJ knew he could count on if anything went wrong. He hadn't kept in close touch during the years after Gene left the rodeo, but he'd known his cousin would be there if he needed him. "I'm sorry I didn't get here earlier, before Gene passed, but…there was EllaJayne and her mama."

Pepper stiffened and not from sorrow. Crap. His smooth tongue had deserted him. He usually wasn't so clueless with women.

She pulled away and turned her head but he saw her wipe at her eyes. "I'm good now," she said with taut determination. "What do we do? Shake hands?"

Chapter Four

Pepper thrust out her hand and stepped away from AJ's heat. Shake hands and move on. That was what she needed to do. Forget she'd broken down in his arms and had liked—way too much—the warm strength of him. He took her hand in his and lingered for a second. She didn't change her grip, making her gaze stay on him. How had she not seen the tiny white scar that stretched up from the corner of his upper lip and another on the outside of his dark brow? His face told her what she needed to know. A rodeo cowboy. They didn't stick around.

"Okay?" he asked with soft gruffness.

She shifted her eyes to a place over his shoulder where she could see the mountains that surrounded Angel Crossing. "I'll get you sitters' names." She could do this. She had to do this for herself, for Faye and for Angel Crossing. They were all counting on her.

As for the other part of this debacle, that he and EllaJayne remain at the ranch? That would be all right, too. No matter there would be months and months of sharing a bathroom, a kitchen. It would be very intimate. No. Cramped. And she'd already gotten a good view of a fit-for-bull-riding cowboy walking around in a towel.

Faye danced onto the patio, bouncing EllaJayne on her hip. "We're going to breathe in the colors."

"Grana," the toddler agreed as they danced off.

Pepper gritted her teeth and glanced at AJ to gauge his reaction. Until she was a teen, Pepper had stayed at the ranch, with Faye homeschooling her. Then she'd gone to public school, where a cowboy wearing anything but Wranglers was cause for comment, and her mother's unusual view of the world after years of living in a commune had mortified Pepper. Now, some days she could appreciate how growing up with Faye had taught her compassion and patience. Angel Crossing needed both. The residents were stubborn about changing anything, even things that would make them healthier.

"All done," Faye said, snuggling her nose against the toddler's. "The blue sky smelled like Aqua Velva and the white clouds made us both think sheets dried outside." The little girl giggled.

"I'll take her now," AJ said, holding his arms out for his daughter.

"Wait," Pepper said. Suddenly, the whole day felt too huge, like something had shifted in the world. Dear Lord, she was starting to sound like Faye. She dug deep for the calm and unemotional Pepper who took over during emergencies. "I want to make sure that we're clear on our responsibilities." AJ nodded. She went through the list, while she kept a professional eye on him. She needed to use her PA Spidey Senses. She could ferret out a lie at twenty paces—

at least that's what she told patients. She just wanted to be certain that he would stick by the agreement.

She looked at him hard. It didn't take a medical degree to interpret his bloodshot eyes or the dark circles underneath. He was exhausted. Why hadn't she noticed that before? She wanted to tell AJ to go get some sleep and she'd take care of everything. But he wasn't her responsibility. She didn't have to care for him. She needed her attorney to straighten out the will. *Where you goin' to find the dinero for that?* Daddy Gene's voice rang in her head. She'd find it because everyone she cared about—which didn't include AJ and his daughter—was counting on her.

PEPPER QUIETLY CLOSED the door to the bedroom she now shared with her mother. AJ and his little girl had been given Faye's room. Faye hadn't minded—she hadn't been spending much time there since Daddy Gene had died. Pepper could only imagine how long tomorrow would feel because last night she hadn't gotten much more than an hour of sleep. Good thing Tuesday was a Dr. Cortez day. It meant her patient load was reasonable.

Pepper headed to the kitchen, not needing to turn on any lights because Faye, as always, had left the house well-lit. Her mother, despite her love of the moon and staying up late, did not like the dark.

Having grown up in a commune, more or less, before Daddy Gene had showed up, Pepper had a high tolerance for sharing space. But sharing the house with AJ made it feel really, really small. Like right now, she could've sworn she smelled his scent of dusty leather, baby powder and...bubble gum? That last was new. It smelled like the flavoring in children's medicine. She moved a little faster. Was Ella-Jayne sick?

AJ stood in the kitchen shirtless, the top button of his jeans undone so she could see the band of his tighty-whities. *Stop looking,* she told herself firmly as she stood in the shadows. She made her gaze move to his hand and the small white bottle he held.

"Is EllaJayne okay?"

"What?" He jerked around, the bottle dropping from his hand, pink syrup spraying everywhere. "Damn it."

"Sorry. Didn't mean to startle you," she mumbled as the syrup dripped down his chest. His well-muscled chest. She had to stop noticing things like that right now. She rushed to the sink for a dishcloth and the cleaning supplies underneath.

"This stuff is sticky. What are you doing awake?" he whispered. She glanced over her shoulder to see him rubbing at the pink drops.

"Here," she said, taking the cloth and wiping at his chest, using her best professional voice and touch. She concentrated on the pink syrup that had caught in the light furring of hair on his chest and the arrow... she looked back up. His pupils had enlarged so that his storm-gray eyes looked black. "Umm...maybe you can do that while I clean up the floor." His hand covered hers. She didn't feel threatened. Instead she felt his warmth and strength, and that was dangerous. Much more than dangerous. That kind of heat could make her...had made her...do stupid things. His mouth softened and the ends curled just a little as his gaze moved over her. She scrutinized his well-defined jaw, hollowed cheeks and the strong column of his neck before focusing on the small white scar that looked doubly pale against his dark skin in the shadows made by the night lights in the kitchen. She wanted to use the tip of her tongue to trace that little ridge of skin and then listen to his breathing catch and his skin pebble and shiver with excitement.

He cleared his throat and the spell of near darkness, his heat and her own addled brain startled her back to reality. She stepped back quickly, not even cringing when she felt the sticky syrup on her sole.

"If you need a refill for EllaJayne, stop by the clinic tomorrow." She turned slowly, refusing to run from the kitchen, even though that's what she should do. "I think you can clean up the rest of the spill."

"It's been years since anyone bathed me, but I think I might like it."

She swung around. He was a macho, jerk bull rider. They were the worst of the worst, Daddy Gene had told her, and he should know since he'd been one of them for a while. Crazy enough to climb on the back of three-quarters of a ton of testosterone-pumped muscle again and again. She needed to remember that about AJ. He was not the man who awkwardly tried to care for his daughter, making her heart go "aww" and her hands itch to smooth the daughter and father's similarly frowning faces.

"Good night," she finally said when he wouldn't stop looking at her.

"You know, your mother told me that she'd seen my arrival—something to do with your sign and a chart."

Pepper pulled in a breath and let it out slowly

through her nose. Why couldn't her mother say normal motherly things, like stay away from my daughter, you no-good rodeo bum? Because that sort of comment had been Daddy Gene's job and he wasn't here. "Faye also believes that a bit of bacon and the water drawn from a well on the new moon cures ingrown toenails." She walked away from him, like a woman who knew where she was going, not one running away from herself.

AJ STARED AT the unfamiliar ceiling, wishing he were in an anonymous hotel room in an anonymous town. His daughter's cranky whimpers would soon be a full-throated I'm-up-and-I-want-attention yell. From his short time as a dad, he'd learned he had another forty-five seconds of peace. He'd take those measly seconds to remind himself he'd climbed on bulls bent on killing him. Dealing with the constant worry and anxiety Baby Girl'd brought into his world was a cake walk, with a huge wobbly cake.

His daughter's cry stopped his thoughts. He had the morning routine down: diaper, T-shirt, socks and then into the car seat so he could use the bathroom without her wandering off. Not that it had worked so well when he'd been fixing the truck. Maybe bungee cords would hold her in the seat? Even he knew that was a bad idea.

He got both of them cleaned up without running into any of the women. Not surprising since EllaJayne liked to wake before the sun. On the bright side, she'd allow him twenty minutes of uninterrupted peace for his first cup of coffee while she sat in his lap sipping her morning milk. It was a part of the day that he could feel almost competent at this fathering thing.

He took both of them out onto the patio to enjoy the cool breeze with EllaJayne wrapped in a little sparkly pony sweatshirt in eye-searing green. He enjoyed the first dark hit of his coffee and Baby Girl's warm head against his shoulder as he watched the pink rays of sun warm the horizon. For those suspended-in-time moments, all was right in the world.

"Oh, you're out here," Pepper said accusingly.

AJ jerked, spilling coffee on himself with a few drops landing on EllaJayne's thick sweatshirt. The little girl squalled. "Shit," he said as he checked her for burns. The hot liquid had splashed across her sweatshirt, which meant he needed to change her. For a toddler who had bad aim with a spoon, Baby Girl was particular about her clothing.

"Did you burn her?"

"No thanks to you," he shot back as he stood with his daughter, who had pitched her sippy cup to the ground where it popped open and spilled. His own jeans were stained with coffee, too, and he knew he'd have a nice red welt. "I'll clean up out here after I change EllaJayne…again."

Pepper opened her mouth to say something then closed it. Her gaze moving from his face downward, skimming quickly over his crotch. "Umm…you okay?" she asked grudgingly.

"Are you going to examine me?" he asked. Her head snapped up and their eyes met. The heat that had filled the space between them last night was back, searing and unexpected. His daughter's head thumped his chest as she wiped her tear-streaked face against his once-clean shirt. Back to reality. "Next time warn me."

He made a strategic retreat. Inside, her dog gave him a cocked-head stare that said: Don't mess with her, buddy.

After he'd redressed himself and his daughter, he returned to the kitchen to make breakfast. He needed to talk to Danny about where to find work. He'd turned down Pepper's half-hearted offer to help him look. His guess was that she hoped if he didn't have a job, he'd move along.

AJ heard the shower running and worked really, really hard to not imagine Pepper in there, naked, wet and soapy. Dear Lord, what was his problem? He heard Baby Girl in her high chair starting to wind up for another good cry. Just as he turned to deal with her, Faye entered the kitchen with a vague smile on her face.

"I dreamed good things for you, Arthur John."

"AJ," he corrected as he pulled out the last container of yogurt for his daughter. His coffee would have to be enough until he could find a grocery store. All the food from the memorial had been eaten over the weekend or was in the freezer. He didn't recognize anything in the fridge. He'd learned already to be very, very wary when Faye offered him a meal.

"I have goat yogurt. Much better than store-bought," she said.

"We're good," AJ said as he offered a spoon of the pink goop. His daughter quickly made her way through the yogurt.

"Neither of you were burned. Good," Pepper said as she walked into the kitchen, giving him a professional once-over glance. Silence filled the room. Both Faye and EllaJayne remained quiet as he and Pepper stared at each other. He couldn't turn his head. Her honey-brown hair lay on her shoulders in damp whirls. The scrubs, shapeless on anyone else, highlighted her curves and showed off the length of her thigh. His gaze landed on her toes, the nails with their cheery flowers and neon color.

He'd promised himself that he'd mend his cowboy ways now that he was a daddy. No more women, at least until he got the hang of being a father, which meant his next date would be around the time Ella-Jayne left for college.

"Do you want me to make you breakfast?" Faye asked Pepper. Finally, AJ could look away.

"I can't be late today. Dr. Cortez is in."

"Oh, my," Faye said and turned to dig in the refrigerator. "Okay. I'll make breakfast for Arthur John."

He'd rather face Tornado the bull again. "I'm good, ma'am."

He quickly got himself and EllaJayne into the truck. He'd stop somewhere for food, maybe take donuts for Danny as payment for his advice. In town, he drove by the Angel Crossing Medical Clinic. Why couldn't he have met Pepper six months ago, before Baby Girl, before his life had gone from fun to grinding responsibility? Six months ago, he'd have taken her out for dancing and drinks and then back to his room. Well, maybe. If he was honest with himself, those anonymous hotel rooms and buckle bunnies had lost their allure. He'd just not figured out what else to do with himself. Now he had a new life, whether he wanted it or not. No use crying over spilled moonshine because he had EllaJayne to care for and was stuck at Santa Faye Ranch. Once he sold the property, he'd have the cash to make sure Baby Girl stayed with him permanently. Of course, until that happened he needed to make money. He didn't care how, really, just so long as it put bills in his pocket and it was legal. *Okay, cowboy*, he told himself. *Saddle up and get to work.*

Chapter Five

Pepper got into her purple SUV to look in on a patient before hitting the clinic. Many of her patients had a standoffish attitude toward her, but she didn't let that stop her from trying to win them over. It was better than when she'd started at the clinic three years ago. From the beginning Daddy Gene had been embraced by Angel Crossing, maybe because he'd leased parts of the property to local ranchers or because he'd been known on the rodeo circuit. She and Faye had never quite fit in, starting with Faye homeschooling her, then sending her to high school with lunches filled with tofu and homemade wheat bread. Between being an EMT after high school and now treating the town, the attitude had been changing. More slowly than she'd like, of course.

After checking her patient, she had plenty of time to get to the clinic, which meant plenty of time to mull over her situation. She figured what she had to work on next was finding day care for AJ's daughter. Could Faye watch the little girl? Probably, except her mother's idea of child rearing and AJ's didn't seem to be in the same universe. Could Pepper watch EllaJayne? Exactly how would she explain that to the doctor who came to the clinic two times a week? It wouldn't come to that. She'd find him a list of women to choose from.

A caregiver by nature, she knew she'd have to make sure she didn't allow herself to get drawn into AJ and his daughter's troubles. And there was trouble there. A cowboy like him didn't set off across country on his own with a toddler if there wasn't some sad story. She'd become a PA to help people. It was why she'd put up the ranch for the grant to start the community garden in the first place.

Even after withdrawing her application, in another three weeks, she'd have her first crop from the greenhouse and cold boxes. She already had plans on how to get the word out and who would get the first veggies. So many of her patients should be on assistance but were too proud. With fresh veggies and eventually fruit, everyone would win. She wanted chickens for eggs, too. First the garden…no, first was getting the ranch into her hands. Daddy Gene had meant for it to go to her and her mother. He'd told them that. His time had just been shorter than they'd all wished and he'd never changed his will. She had to believe he wouldn't have been upset that she was going to fight AJ for the ranch.

Could she just threaten to go to court? Her attorney seemed like a go-getter. AJ, with his drawl and cowboy swagger, wouldn't know what hit him.

"Knock, knock," a woman's voice said as the door opened. "I know you're not officially open but…"

"Not a problem. Come in, Lavonda."

"I wouldn't be here for myself, but I live with a big

stubborn Scot who is about to die from coughing. I think you saw him, didn't you?"

"Yes. And I told him if the cough didn't clear up to come in."

"Silly you." Lavonda Leigh Kincaid laughed. "I would think that you've dealt with enough cowboys to know the routine."

Lavonda was Mayor Danny Leigh's sister, and newly wed to Professor of Archeology Jones Kincaid. She'd also taken over a company that provided guided tours of the Arizona desert. She'd been friendly with Pepper, explaining that women under the age of sixty in this town needed to bond together since there were so few of them.

"The routine being that unless he can't lift his head from where it hit the ground after he fell down, he's fine?"

"Something like that. Really, if you could just give me something strong enough to knock him out, he'd get better. He just needs to sleep for a couple of days."

"Let me write a prescription for cough syrup. It's not fancy but it'll work and better yet, it should make him drowsy. Keep him from driving, operating machinery, and so on while he's taking this."

"Bless you." Lavonda watched Pepper write up the prescription. "How are you doing?"

"I didn't catch whatever the professor has."

"That's not what I meant. The memorial. The relative who inherited the ranch."

Pepper reminded herself that she really did love Angel Crossing even if the gossip mill would give the NSA a run for its money. "It's been tough. But having the service… I don't know. It…it gets better every day."

"And the situation with the ranch?"

That Pepper really didn't want to talk about.

Lavonda went on, "Your community garden would make such a difference. Of course, it would give people food, but I also think that it could be a way to get and keep the under-sixty crowd living here. I did a little research and community gardens are a thing."

Not surprising Lavonda had done research. Before moving to Angel Crossing, she'd been a PR mogul… or something like that. "I really think it's more about feeding people and giving others a chance to create businesses."

"I agree. Is there a way to work with Gene's… cousin, right? Maybe he'd give you a chance to pay for the ranch over time? Or something like that?"

Pepper handed over the prescription and shrugged. "I'm working on it."

"You know, my sister's brother-in-law is an attorney in Tucson, if you need a legal opinion."

"Already got that but thanks."

"I want to help. The garden is a good idea."

"I thought so, but it's causing nothing but headaches. Would you believe that I've got to find day care now? And on the cheap and top-notch."

"Everybody wants something for nothing."

Lavonda's gaze immediately went to Pepper's waistline. "Not for me. Good God, no. That's just what I'd need." Another reason to stay away from AJ. He apparently easily made babies. "It's Daddy Gene's cousin." That sentence was harder to say than she'd imagined. "He's—"

"The ranch stealer."

Lavonda went up three notches in Pepper's book. "He will be the new owner and he's got a little girl who needs looking after."

"I saw them at the memorial. If you can't find anyone, let me know. I can probably squeeze in a few hours here and there. Why isn't he looking?"

"He's out on the job search and I said I'd help." Lavonda didn't need to know any secrets that weren't general knowledge.

"Nice of you, considering."

Pepper just nodded.

"I'd better get going so I can dose up my cowboy, but seriously, call me either for the attorney or the babysitting."

"I will," Pepper said and meant it. Angel Crossing had changed. She needed to let go of some of the snubs and name-calling. That had been so long ago. Look how people had come out to the memorial and brought food. Plus, she thought she and Lavonda just might become friends. That would be nice.

"GOING TO COURT is the wrong path," Faye said later that night when they were cleaning up the dishes. "It will only lead to disaster."

Her mother didn't think AJ inheriting their ranch was a disaster and yet for her, Pepper calling an attorney was a problem. "You need some Windex to clean up your window into the future, Faye. I'm protecting you, me and Angel Crossing."

"It's still the wrong way. Karma will get you."

"You always say that."

"She always says what?" AJ asked as he came into the kitchen.

"Nothing," Pepper answered, giving her mother "the look"—the one Pepper had perfected for recalcitrant patients.

"I should have a job by the end of the week. Do you have caregivers for me to check out?"

"You know, this really should be your job. I work full time plus." She wanted to be sure that he understood what he'd asked of her.

"Do you have a list?" His storm-gray gaze stayed glued to her face.

"I have better things to do with my time." That was true, except she had Lavonda and a couple of other leads. Why was she being such a pain about this? She opened her mouth to give him the names.

"We shook on it."

It wasn't the words. It was the self-righteous tone. "Only until this entire situation gets overturned by the courts." Damn it. She hadn't meant to tip her hand. Why did he get her so mad? She was the calm one. Faye was the one who let things slip out. Faye was the one ruled by emotion.

"The will is legal."

"And you know that how? Seems like you fell one too many times on your head."

"Children, children," Faye said, drifting into the space between them. "You mustn't use your energies on arguments."

"Faye's right," AJ said, crossing his arms over his chest. "You'd be wasting your time and energy, fighting the will. It's airtight. Gene left me the ranch."

AJ didn't raise his voice. He didn't need to. She

read his anger in every solid inch of him. None of it stopped her from saying, "So says the man who is the will's beneficiary."

Faye waved her hand, making her bracelets clink. "We are all beneficiaries. Gene always thought of others." Her mother paused and cocked her head. "I can almost hear him saying: 'Pepper, face the facts and don't hire a snake-oil attorney.'"

Pepper could feel AJ's gaze and knew that it would have pity and maybe a little bit of smugness. Faye brought that out in others. Early on and even after Daddy Gene entered their lives, Pepper knew it was up to her to make sure that the practicalities of daily life got taken care of. Like now, if she didn't fight the will, Faye and Pepper would be homeless, abandoning Faye's Beauties and living on a rural PA's meager salary.

"So are you going to listen to your mother?" AJ asked.

She searched his face and found something there that might have been laughter or... "I always listen to my mother, but I'm also a grown woman and know our rights. We have a right to this ranch and my town has a right to good, healthy food. You aren't going to stop me from getting both of those things. No matter what karma I have to defy."

"KARAOKE?" AJ ASKED as he read the flyer behind the bar.

"Country-western karaoke," Danny said, lifting two fingers for the bartender to refill their beers.

AJ considered telling Danny no and going home to Baby Girl, but today had sucked big-time. He'd driven to the mine two towns over and stopped at four ranches. No work for a former bull rider and sometime-wrangler. Everyone had been nice and polite, but that didn't pay the bills.

"You think they need help?" he asked Danny, lifting his shoulder to the bar. He was only half kidding.

"Woman-run and woman-owned." The mugs of beer were set in front of them, and they sipped in quiet for a few moments. "There's a prize for the best karaoke singer."

"The hell you say."

"Come on. You're the one who said you needed to make money."

"At a job, not making a fool of myself singin' 'Crazy' or 'Friends in Low Places.'"

"Just trying to help. How's everything else going? Settling in okay?"

"As long as I don't let Faye cook for me, everything's good. Still don't know why Gene didn't change his will."

Danny shrugged. "He was your cousin, right? And you did save him at that rodeo. When was that? Eight? Nine years ago?"

"I was just at the right place, that's all. My God, I didn't even make it out here to see him after he got so sick."

"You called. He understood. It wasn't like you didn't come because you were shacked up with some buckle bunny. You were fighting to get your daughter. Don't look a gift ranch in the mouth."

"I'm not, just wondering." They sipped their beers in silence again. "Since she's watching my daughter tonight, guess I should ask what Pepper's story is?"

"I wondered how long it'd be until you asked about her." Danny grinned knowingly.

AJ wanted to take back the question and walk out of the bar. He went cowboy-quiet.

"I haven't been here that long but I understand Faye and Gene came drifting into town when Pepper was six." Danny paused, took a gulp of beer and went on. "You know that she and Gene hooked up at the commune where Faye grew up, free love and all that. Pepper was born there. No one knows who Pepper's biological father is. Why Faye and Gene came to Angel Crossing is a mystery. She insists there are vortexes here like up in Sedona. If there are, it hasn't brought us the tourists and the money like that place."

This explained a lot. "Pepper wants to start a commune at the ranch?"

"Nah. Just a community garden. She wants to grow fresh veggies to give or sell at low cost and then expand to rent plots for residents to grow their own for themselves or to sell. That's how she'll have a bit of income beyond grants and donations. There are a lot of older folks and proud poor ones who need just a little help. It's not such a bad idea."

AJ couldn't feel guilty for putting that plan in jeopardy. He had his daughter to worry about. Tonight he didn't want to talk about the ranch or any of the responsibilities that went with it. He wanted to be a cowboy, here to enjoy his beer, the music and maybe a cowgirl or two. AJ looked around the bar. Not many people, but then, it was a weeknight.

"If you're looking for work, I keep in touch with the guys from the circuit. I'm sure I could find some place that needs a wrangler or a rider."

AJ shook his head. He didn't want to go on the road and leave his daughter. That's why he'd given up the only job he'd ever wanted. He'd not been in the big money but he'd made a living. There was an ache in his back and hip, but that was to be expected and it hadn't been enough to keep him off a bull. "Can't leave my daughter."

Danny nodded his head. "You miss it?"

AJ could tell there was something in his friend's voice that made it more than a casual question. "I'm responsible for my daughter. She's got to come first."

"Seems like everyone is getting hitched and having babies."

AJ couldn't imagine his friend pining for the settled life. On the other hand, he had come to Angel Crossing and become mayor. AJ couldn't have imagined that when the two of them were rippin' it up in every honky-tonk from San Antonio to Laramie. "We're all getting older," AJ said lamely.

"Not that old. Let's do a shot," Danny said and motioned to the bartender again.

AJ shook his head. "I've got to get going, man." He stood up and for just a moment he longed again for the days when he would have stayed until the bartender kicked him out, maybe leaving with a woman who was soft and willing. Had that really just been last year? He clapped Danny on the shoulder. "Drink one for me and we'll go out another night to celebrate when I get my new job."

DARN. LIGHTS WERE still on in the ranch house. He didn't want to talk with anyone. He wanted to crawl into bed and hope tomorrow was better. His back and hip ached after being forced to change a tire on the pickup along the side of the dark road. All of it was a reminder that his life was quickly sliding toward crap. Could he hold out until the ranch was his? He had to.

He stopped inside the door, listening. He didn't hear a TV, the baby, Faye or Pepper—who'd convinced him she could deal with his daughter's bedtime. He pulled off his boots and snuck to the kitchen. He'd get a glass of water, take an aspirin so he could sleep until the Baby Girl pre-dawn alarm clock went off.

He slowly opened the door to his room so he'd not disturb EllaJayne. Shi…crap…da…darn. There on his bed was Pepper herself with a wide-awake EllaJayne in her arms. The baby was contenting herself with playing at opening and closing the snaps on Pepper's cowgirl shirt. When she wasn't in scrubs, Pepper wore the cowgirl uniform well. He'd noticed that before, especially her second-skin jeans.

He could pick up the little girl without seeing or touching anything on Pepper he shouldn't. He tiptoed toward the bed. EllaJayne's eyes narrowed. Of course, his daughter wasn't thrilled to see Daddy. She'd rather hug Oggie than him. Where was the stuffed animal? He looked around and then saw it squashed between Pepper's arm and breast. Lucky dog.

"Come on, EllaJayne," he whispered as he reached out his hands slowly. "Time for night-night." He held his breath as the little girl shook her head. If he grabbed her quick enough, she'd be in his arms before she could make a noise. He reached forward, thinking that he'd ease Oggie out before swooping in for his daughter. He leaned over, breathing slowly and calmly, like he was working with a skittish horse. He caught a scent of baby powder mixed with lemon and clove. He leaned in farther, his hand hovering just over the dog. EllaJayne stared at him without blinking. He touched Oggie. She grasped the toy and yelled. Pepper's eyes popped open, just as his hand got squashed between her breast and the stuffed animal.

"What are you doing?" she asked as she sat up, pulled away and grasped his squawking daughter to her.

"Putting EllaJayne to bed," he said, keeping a wary eye on the suddenly quiet girl.

Pepper stood, her lush mouth transformed into a straight, thin line. She handed over the girl and walked out.

His daughter cooperated and went into her bed without a peep. AJ wanted or maybe needed to apologize to Pepper. "EllaJayne is down for the night," he said when he found her in the kitchen where she was putting away dishes. "Thanks again for watching her." She didn't look any less strained or annoyed. "And, well, sorry…about earlier."

She nodded. She didn't move. He didn't move. The tension in the kitchen neared the twanging tightness of a guitar string. He had to break it somehow. "So," he said. "I'm going to have a snack."

She still didn't move from the drain board. He dug into the back of the cupboard and pulled out a box of Fiddle Faddle.

"Where did you get that?" she asked.

"I bought it."

"I know you bought it. How did you hide it? Faye always finds my stash."

"Your stash?"

"She always finds my Cadbury fruit-and-nut bars. No matter where I hide them. It's like she's got radar. Daddy Gene always hid Devil Dogs."

"I didn't know I had to hide stuff."

"Share and I won't rat you out," she said and held out her hand.

He offered the open box to her. "There's a place near to home that makes better caramel corn than this but a beggar can't be a complainer."

"If you say so. This is pretty darned good." She popped a piece of caramel-covered popcorn in her mouth and chewed in obvious bliss.

He would have laughed if that picture didn't make him think of the brief flash of heat he'd felt when his hand had cupped her breast as he'd worked to get Oggie. He wasn't proud of it, but there it was. He may have, possibly without conscious thought, copped a feel.

"You can't distract me anymore," she said as she walked to the sink and turned on the tap. "We need to talk about—" She stopped, gazing out the window over the sink, then she turned and ran out the back door.

What the hell? He looked out the window and saw flames. Crap. He followed her, yelling, "Pepper, don't."

"My plants," she yelled. He was nearly to her.

"I'm calling 9-1-1, then we'll get the hose."

She stopped and turned to him, her face eerily illuminated by the flames. "The plants...the greenhouse..."

"I know. Go get the hose. I'll call." She started toward the greenhouse and its attached shed, but the flames were higher than the nearby barn. He grabbed her arm to stop her. She seemed to be in a trance. "You don't want the barn to catch fire. The greenhouse is gone."

"Oh, my God, Faye was right. Karma doesn't like attorneys."

Chapter Six

Pepper concentrated on watching the volunteer firefighters roll up their hoses. It had taken them less than ten minutes to put out the fire. In all, the greenhouse and shed couldn't have been burning for more than twenty minutes and it was all gone. The flames had been hot enough to twist the metal and burn up all the tubes and the electronic control system.

"Sorry," the fire chief said, followed by nods from the other volunteers, most of whom had been treated at the clinic.

"Thanks for trying to save it." She'd known from the moment she and AJ had run outside that the greenhouse was a goner. She looked around for him. He stood with a small cluster of men. She moved her gaze away from AJ, where it had been landing far too often. He'd pitched in as the firefighters had sprayed the greenhouse, then used rakes and long poles to poke at the charred remains so they were sure no spark or ember was left.

"We'll be out of here soon. Chief Rudy will be by tomorrow to check, but it doesn't look like arson to me. I'd say electrical or maybe from compost. You'd be amazed how quickly that stuff can catch fire."

Pepper stared at the charred remains of her dreams. She sounded a lot more like Faye than herself, which gave her an idea of how crazy upset she was. She'd face it all tomorrow—including the insurance company— when she wasn't exhausted. Then she'd come up with a way to salvage her garden and her plan for Angel Crossing and her mother.

"At least the barn didn't catch fire," AJ said, his drawl thick and his words soft.

"Yeah, at least."

"It was just plants and they weren't even that big." He stood beside her, both of them looking over the ashes, white-green in the weak light from the old dusk-to-dawn lamp crookedly attached to the barn.

"You'd think that, you…cowboy jerk." She wanted to punch him, too, but this wasn't elementary school. *Cowboy jerk*? Really, that was the best insult she could come up with?

"I'll ignore that," he said easily.

Why was he being nice? She couldn't keep up a good head of anger if he was nice to her. If he didn't stop it, she'd be crying. He pulled her without warning into a one-armed hug. She stiffened. She wouldn't be coddled or humored. She was an adult, as much a tough-as-horseshoes cowgirl as anyone else. Daddy Gene had told her she had to be the one to live in the real world, make sure the bills were paid because Faye was…Faye. Pepper had done it whenever Gene was on the road or had gone off to find work. She'd made the same promise when he knew his disease had come roaring back and he was dying.

AJ's words drifted over her head, making the hair

move. "I *can* be a jerk, just ask around. But not to-night."

She relaxed into his embrace, feeling surrounded not only by his warmth but something more, a comfort that surprised her. She wanted to lean into him, let him take on her fear, disappointment and anger. Just for ten seconds. Yes, for ten seconds, she could be defeated and let someone else take on her responsibilities. She reached her arm around him, pressing her face into his shoulder, into the muscled solidity of him. Substantial and safe.

She counted off the seconds in her head but somewhere around six her brain just stopped and she only felt. He held her more tightly against him. She didn't pull away. She wanted to melt into him.

"Pepper?"

She glanced up at him. His gaze roamed over her face. She tipped up her chin, offering herself to him.

No. She needed to step away. She needed to—

His mouth came down on hers, feather-light in its touch. Testing and tasting her. She tasted back, then opened her mouth on a deep inhale of need and desire that ran through her, racing from the notch at the base of her throat south, settling hotly between her thighs. She should pull away. That would be smart. Instead, she turned into his one-armed embrace, reaching up and around his wide, solid shoulders, digging her fingers into the bunching muscles, enjoying the strength and resilience of his flesh. His arms wrapped around her. They fit just right, everything aligning as it should, as if they had been a couple for decades with every curve and hollow matched to make something that was greater than just the two of them.

His hands moved under her ponytail to pull her mouth more firmly against his, urging her to open to him further. She did and the explosion of taste, feeling and heat went straight to her knees, which wobbled with the unexpected but not unwelcome rush of lust. Lordy be. She reveled for long moments in the heat and want of that dance of their tongues but finally made herself pull her head away. She didn't move out of his loose embrace, though, slowing her breathing even as she enjoyed the hot scent of him. His gaze didn't leave her face, searching but not demanding. At last, she stepped out of his arms.

"Thanks. Good night." She walked with purpose back into the house, where the bright lights and Faye's questions would wipe away the kiss. Just part of the shock of the fire, she told herself in her best medical-professional voice. Nothing was going on between her and the cowboy. Nothing. He and his little girl were not her future. She would have a community garden and settle down with a man who held the same values as she did and understood how important it was to sacrifice for the community. Someone sort of like Danny Leigh. He'd given up a lot to become mayor. Yeah, that was the kind of man for her. Not AJ McCreary, a broken-down bull rider who'd sell off her ranch.

"AJ has Aries rising, a fire sign," Faye said to Pepper when she came into the kitchen.

"Are you saying the fire was his fault?"

"Of course not. He would never do anything like

that. I meant that he is a good complement to your air sign. You'll feed his fire."

Pepper stared at her mother. The woman must have seen the kiss. "AJ is an unemployed cowboy with a baby and an attitude, who will soon be stealing our ranch."

Faye reached out her hands with her palms toward Pepper, reading her aura, something her mother insisted she could do. "Don't think too much, sweetie. Allow your heart, not your stethoscope, to make your decision. Have a cup of the yam root tea and then go to bed. Everything will work out." Faye drifted out of the kitchen. Pepper couldn't go to bed yet, not with the fire department still working.

"I would've told you that the idiots in Angel Crossing can take care of themselves. Your job was to settle down and give me grandbabies." A voice drifted through her mind sounding a lot like Daddy Gene at his most exasperated. She was going to put that down to stress. Tomorrow she'd come up with a plan that would save her garden and Faye's future. Daddy Gene had been right to expect Pepper to care for her mother. That was the way it worked between the two of them, which meant she had to get rid of the cowboy and his claim.

AJ USED BABY GIRL as a shield when he walked into the kitchen the morning after the fire. He wasn't sure exactly what to expect from Pepper. He certainly didn't believe she'd want a repeat of the kiss. He had enough experience with women to know that. He also thought he might need to apologize, which he would do if he had to—even though he hadn't done anything she hadn't wanted to.

No one was in the kitchen, despite EllaJayne allowing him to sleep in until a time when other humans usually got up. Everything was neat and clean, not one coffee-mug ring. His daughter wriggled in his arms, letting him know that her patience had worn thin. She was hungry and he'd better insert food quickly. He went through the morning routine and still not one of the Bourne women appeared. Finally, both he and EllaJayne had eaten, and he'd drank two cups of strong coffee.

He walked outside with Baby Girl on his hip. Pepper stood by the heap of ashes that had been the greenhouse. His daughter flapped her arms, holding out Oggie, babbling and pointing at Pepper. She seemed to be more enthused seeing the stranger than she was to see him. That could be because he washed her face, and made her do things like eat eggs and sit in her high chair.

He heard the bark just before he felt the solid weight of Butch landing against his legs. At least one living being on this ranch appreciated him. The dog danced around his feet as AJ moved toward Pepper. The woman looked determined—no sign of the vulnerable person she'd been last night. Phone to her ear, she paced through the ashes. Butch brought AJ a rock to throw. AJ sent it sailing and the dog raced after it. EllaJayne jabbered loudly in his ear as she pointed at Pepper, who continued to pace. He understood about every tenth word his daughter said, so he knew enough to take her to Pepper. He set EllaJayne on the ground, putting out his hand so she could totter around while continuing to wave Oggie to Pepper, who gave them a quick nod. Butch came back with a new rock. He waited, sitting on his haunches until he caught sight of the moving stuffed animal. AJ saw the direction of his gaze and moved to grab it before the dog lunged. Too late. Butch nabbed Oggie and raced away. EllaJayne screamed. AJ closed his eyes as a sharp pain radiated from his back to his brain. The stupid reach for the toy had tweaked his back. He hadn't been doing his physical therapy exercises, the ones meant to loosen his muscles and keep them from knotting up. When his back acted up, his hip would start throbbing and soon his shoulder would join in. Darn it. He finally opened his eyes as the sharp pain dialed back.

Now the pain moved to his heart as he saw the shiny tracks on EllaJayne's face, her eyes swimming with tears and her brow scrunched in hurt. He whistled sharply for the dog who came trotting back to Pepper instead of him. She stuck the phone in her pocket and then pointed to the ground. Butch dropped Oggie a good twenty feet from AJ.

"Look, baby," he said to his daughter. "Butch brought back Oggie. He's fine. Let's go get him." He didn't know if he could pick her up right now. She wasn't heavy, but pain shot from his back and down his leg. His daughter toddled, then collapsed, pulling on AJ's arm, and his back chose that moment to freeze into a sheet of pain that sent him to his knees beside EllaJayne.

"Oggie," his daughter screamed, her little arm shooting out toward Pepper and the stuffed animal. AJ worked to get his breath and stand up. If he was lucky, the muscles would unclench without him having to lie flat out on his back on the ground.

"He's fine, EllaJayne. Butch didn't hurt him," Pepper said in soothing tones as she approached the two of them. AJ's back muscles clamped down again, his breath stopping for a second. When the spasm loosened, he made himself look at her and even smiled.

"Thanks." Another thirty seconds and he'd move, he assured himself.

Pepper looked at him intently, her eyes scanning up and down his body, before turning to EllaJayne. She handed over the stuffed animal. "See. He's fine." The little girl clasped the pile of balding fur to her chest, then gave a dark-eyed glare at Butch. If AJ had had the breath, he would have laughed because that glare was pure Nanny McCreary, his great-grandmother, who'd been the terror of the clan. No one crossed that woman. She'd kept the family fed and on its land through the Great Depression with willpower and a shotgun.

"Oggie," EllaJayne finally said, still hugging her toy. "Bad Butch." At least that was what AJ thought she said. With the throbbing pain now settling into his back, it was tough to think about much more than getting to the house and finding a flat surface to stretch out on and a bottle of pills to take. Only he couldn't knock himself out because he had EllaJayne and calls to make. He took a deep breath and levered himself slowly and painfully to his feet, keeping his gaze on the ground. He didn't want to see anything like pity in Pepper's eyes. "I'll need the names of the sitters and directions," he said, to give himself something else to focus on.

"I've got the insurance to deal with today but come

with me into the clinic and let me check you out. It's obvious you're in pain."

"Just an old injury. It's nothing. It'll only take you a minute to get me the names," he said tightly, feeling the hot wave of clenching pain starting again at his hips. He needed to relax or it would never unknot. He needed to get horizontal, too. Crap. That one small thought had him remembering their kiss and the promise of the heat they would have generated if they'd gotten horizontal together. At least imagining that made him forget about his back for a moment or two. He straightened a fraction of an inch and the stiffness eased. "I plan to go out on interviews tomorrow. I need the sitter hired today." He looked at his daughter happily sitting on her once-clean bottom in the dusty yard, sifting gravel and dirt over her legs. Leaning over the tub to wash her again wasn't going to happen. He'd figure something out because he and EllaJayne needed to make a good impression on the sitter. "Come on, Baby Girl," he said to her. His daughter looked up, her face marred by the now dirty streaks of her earlier tears.

"Up," she said, lifting her arms. "Want up."

No way could he do that. "Not now. You walk. Get Oggie and come." He saw her lip start to stick out, ready for a long pout. "You can play horsey," he promised. His daughter loved sitting on his saddle that had a place in the corner of the room until AJ could clean out the barn enough for his equipment. Finally, Ella-Jayne pushed herself to her feet and started to walk like a drunken sailor toward the house. "I want to leave for town as soon as I have the names," he said to Pepper before walking away.

Twenty-five minutes later, EllaJayne was as clean as a wet washcloth could make her. His back had settled into a dull throb that he might keep under control with double doses of aspirin and stretches. He'd ridden with worse.

"Pepper," he called, Ella Jayne toddling beside him into the kitchen. She was there, the morning sun highlighting the golden red in her hair and making her eyes glow. Dear Lord, her earthy beauty knocked the breath out of him, but in the good way, like a beautiful sunset or a first kiss. "Baby Girl is cleaned up, aren't you?" he asked his daughter so he had to turn from Pepper. He needed to get some distance. "We're ready to go find a sitter."

"I didn't have much time…"

Her voice drifted off but he resisted checking out what had shut her up. He stared at the top of his daughter's dark head. "As soon as you get me the names, we'll be out of your hair."

AJ HAD THE two measly names she'd finally given him and his daughter strapped in her seat when a semi pulled up with pallets of plants on its trailer. What the heck? This must be for her garden, but what had she been thinking? She'd ordered enough plants to feed the entire state. Not his business, he reminded himself. He walked over to talk with the driver who jumped out of the cab.

"You order a thousand King Kale plants?"

"That wouldn't be me. Could it be Pepper Bourne?"

The guy looked at the paperwork. "Angel Crossing Community Garden."

Butch raced over barking, and AJ heard the llamas

and alpacas calling out. He couldn't bend to catch the dog's collar, so he clicked his fingers and pointed to his side. Butch circled him once, then plopped his hairy butt in the dirt.

"What's going on... My plants?" Pepper was ten feet away. He saw her eyes go wide. "I didn't order—"

"You Angel Crossing Community Garden?" the driver asked, approaching her with the clipboard as Butch continued to race around again, barking like a maniac.

"Butch, hush," Pepper said ineffectually, and then to the man with the clipboard, "I ordered kale but—"

"One thousand King Kale, five hundred Queen Mustard and another thousand Marquis Artichokes."

"I only ordered a dozen of each plant."

"Nope. See here?" He tried to show her the clipboard.

AJ joined them. "Is there a problem with the order?"

Pepper said tightly. "I never ordered that amount. That would be enough to feed the city of Phoenix."

"I have the invoice," the man said just as Butch's barking went from loud to shrill. The sound of hooves pounded nearby. They all turned to see the herd of alpacas and llamas stampeding to the low trailer of plants. The animals nearly trampled each other getting to the greenery.

Pepper turned, waving her arms at the creatures to shoo them away. Not one furry beast paid attention. "Get out," she shouted. The man with the clipboard stood frozen to the spot as Butch raced around, deciding he really was a herding dog. He barked and nipped at the llamas and alpacas.

Pepper yelled, "Faye, get your animals. Now."

AJ moved as quickly as he could when he saw that the creatures weren't going to be moved along. He was stopped short and sent to the ground by a muscle spasm that froze his legs and took away their strength. The truck driver continued to stand with his mouth open.

"Oh, dear," Faye said, "My Beauties are being bad today."

"Lady," the driver yelled over the racket. "Get them out of there or I'm calling the cops. They're going to ruin my other deliveries."

"You shouldn't have tempted them," Faye chided.

AJ caught his breath between the muscle spasms and said, "Get in the truck and drive away before they eat everything."

The driver took the advice. The truck started up. Startled, the animals scattered and stampeded off into the desert with Butch and Pepper racing after them.

Faye stood quietly. "I tried to warn her about the attorney. She always did have to figure out things the hard way."

Chapter Seven

Worrying over her patients at the clinic, working on a way to get AJ to come in for an exam on his back and hip as well as finally getting to making a longer list of child care alternatives for EllaJayne were preferable mental exercises to going over the disasters Pepper'd had at the ranch, culminating with the destroyed plants last week. She shoveled in her yogurt to make up for the missed lunch, which she'd spent talking with the insurance company...again. The greenhouse and damaged plants weren't covered. Every day got her deeper in debt with no end in sight. Maybe she should have listened more seriously to Faye and her predictions on how the universe viewed their situation and Pepper's calls to the attorney. It didn't seem fair or right since she'd only called in the law to look out for everyone's best interests—except AJ's.

"Mrs. Carmichael is here. Need you in Exam Two," Claudette said and looked almost sorry for interrupting Pepper's furtive meal.

No rest for the wicked or those who went against the universe. She threw away the yogurt and focused on her next patient. She'd take care of everything else later. Although…perhaps Mrs. Carmichael might be a good choice as a caregiver for EllaJayne. By working out a deal with the grandmotherly Mrs. Carmichael, like a couple of free appointments and insulin samples, Pepper might get on the universe's and AJ's good side.

PEPPER WATCHED ELLAJAYNE babbling to Oggie from her car seat in the back of the purple SUV. AJ, desperate and harried, had called her early in the day asking her to pick up the little girl from the high-priced day care near to Tucson. Lucky for him, they'd had an extra car seat for her to borrow. She hadn't even had a chance to tell him about Mrs. Carmichael, who already looked after her own grandchildren and was happy to take on another little one—and at a bargain-basement price. She was perfect. Pepper loved when things worked out. She'd bask in the glow of this success before tackling the will and the damage at the ranch. "Right, EllaJayne," she said to the little girl.

"Oggie," she yelled in agreement, shaking her stuffed animal.

Pepper smiled. "Oggie and you will love Mrs. Carmichael. She makes the best cookies, which might be why she can't keep her blood sugar under control. I should look for low sugar recipes for her. Good idea, EllaJayne." It was kind of nice to have another person in the car, even if the toddler's conversation was limited.

"I wonder what Faye's making for dinner. It doesn't matter. I have a secret stash of sausages in the back of the freezer that I'm going to cook to celebrate." She thought her triumphant solution deserved a special dinner. Faye would fuss about the meat for ten minutes tops, Pepper predicted. Her mother tried to be a good vegetarian, but she rarely turned down pork—and pork in the form of sausages was irresistible to Faye.

As she lifted EllaJayne from the car seat, Pepper glared at the jerk-face llamas and alpacas placidly hanging out in the corral. Her mother still insisted on calling them her Beauties, despite the destruction they'd caused with their stampede. Pepper would be paying off that stunt for who knew how long and how far back it would set her plans for the garden. She'd play Scarlett O'Hara on that—tomorrow was another day. Tonight she'd celebrate her one victory. Mrs. Carmichael would get her points with AJ, which had nothing to do with what had happened after the fire and everything to do with the agreement they had.

"Down. Want down," EllaJayne insisted, drumming her feet against Pepper's thigh. She wasn't falling for that. If she put the toddler down, she'd be off and into something. She knew only too well now how AJ could have lost track of the little girl on that first day they'd met. "Boot," the little girl insisted and pointed. Pepper followed her finger. Butch was racing toward them, panting happily. He barked and ran in circles around Pepper as she tried to walk inside. He didn't quiet until EllaJayne was on the ground and he'd sniffed her over, licked her face and then knocked her down with his enthusiasm. Pepper waited for the little girl to cry. Instead, she giggled and shouted, "Boot, Boot, Boot." Apparently that was toddler for *Butch*.

"You look much better," Faye said as she walked calmly into the chaos on the porch.

"I'm cooking dinner, and we're having sausages on the grill." Her mother protested for eight minutes and then agreed it was probably for the best since AJ needed extra protein. Pepper didn't ask why. When Faye made those kinds of pronouncements, it was always better to not know why. She made her way to the kitchen listening to the dog, her mother and the little girl play in the living room.

When the food was ready, EllaJayne pounded a spoon against the table, giggling at the barking Butch. Finally, twenty minutes after the sausages came off the grill and with no call from AJ, Pepper said, "Let's eat," putting a cheery lilt into her voice for the little girl. She'd only agreed to the day care pickup. AJ shouldn't assume that because she and her mother were female, they were built-in babysitters. She focused on dinner. It had been a long time since they'd had such a treat. She'd been given the sausages by a patient, who used a secret family recipe to make them. They were nearly as precious as gold in the Angel Crossing bartering system that was used for everything from an office visit to a bag of coffee at the general store. They were bliss on her tongue. She glanced over at the suddenly quiet EllaJayne who was trying to give Butch her sausage.

"No, you don't," Pepper said, swooping in to snatch the meat and clear off the little girl's plate. She immediately started to wail, until Pepper plunked down a bowl of yogurt—not Faye's but handmade at a small dairy that had started up in the next town—along with fresh fruit. Pepper began feeding her. EllaJayne didn't have the coordination to use the spoon fast enough for her yogurt greed.

"You loved yogurt, too," Faye said, "although cheese curds were your favorite. There was a dairy woman from Wisconsin who lived at Dove's Paradise."

Pepper remembered quite a bit about Dove's Paradise, the commune that she'd lived in with her mother and her mother's parents.

"You know," Faye started, "the universe had a plan when Gene's truck broke down at our door that day."

Pepper had heard this story, but there was a comfort in listening again to how Daddy Gene's radiator had leaked, he'd stopped for water and her mother had been there. Faye insisted their water signs had immediately recognized each other. Daddy Gene had said all he'd noticed was her halter top and Daisy Duke shorts. They'd gotten together then, but Daddy Gene had been on the road nearly all the time. It had been two more years before he bought the place outside Angel Crossing and invited Faye to join him, telling her that he'd already named the ranch for her, so she had to agree. Pepper felt tears gathering. She couldn't believe he was gone.

"Daddy," EllaJayne yelled.

Pepper started, spilling yogurt. She looked but didn't see AJ. "Not yet, baby," Pepper said, offering another spoonful. The little girl shook her head and Butch barked.

"They must hear something," Faye said serenely. "I'll make AJ a plate so it's ready for him. I feel he needs a little pampering."

Pepper wondered if something in the air was turning everyone—except her—into a nutcase. "Are you done?" she asked EllaJayne.

"Want Daddy. More yogurt." The toddler smacked the table. Butch went into another frenzy of barking.

Pepper lifted the wriggling child from her chair and carried her back to the tub for a wash down. Both yogurt and potato salad decorated her hair. Butch joined them despite the fact he hated the tub as much as he hated getting his feet wet—lucky for her and him that they lived in the desert.

She'd only gotten EllaJayne's shoes and socks off before her mother called for her. Something in her voice caught Pepper's attention. She picked up Ella-Jayne and went to the kitchen.

"What, Faye?" she asked.

"Daddy," EllaJayne screamed in her ear. The little girl was right this time. AJ was standing beside Faye. Then he turned around slowly, painfully and she knew why Faye had sounded odd.

AJ's ACHING CHEEK and back stopped him from smiling at his little girl—who for the first time seemed happy to see him. He noted the concern and something more in Pepper's eyes before her gaze traveled over him like a doctor. He opened his mouth, but she beat him to it.

"Don't move until I can check you over. Faye, take EllaJayne." She handed off his daughter, who snuggled into Faye with her thumb in her mouth.

"I'm fine."

"That's a lie." She stared hard at his face, then turned to her mother. "Get EllaJayne ready for *b-e-d.*"

Every creature at the ranch knew his little girl

hated the word *bed*. AJ allowed the homey smells of food and baby powder to waft over him, erasing a fraction of the day's disasters. Still, he had a job, even if it was temporary.

"Sit," Pepper said.

"I just need aspirin, a beer and dinner."

"Sit first. I want to look at that cheek and where else? Your back?"

He nodded carefully because the muscles in his neck were the consistency of concrete. Soon he'd be frozen in place from the tip of his head to his heels. He hadn't had spasms like this since he'd tweaked his back two years ago. Of course, he hadn't been regularly hauling hay and feed or helping a reluctant heifer give birth—her bucking and twisting had ended with him flat on his back, a bruise on his cheek. Although when she'd first smacked him with her thrashing head, he'd thought she'd broken his entire face.

Pepper's touch, strong but light, quickly traveled over his body. Professional but not without sympathy. When he'd gone to the ER or hospital before, they'd treated him like an inanimate object who periodically made noise.

"When did you injure your back?"

"While ago," he hissed out as she touched a particularly sore spot. It might have been where he'd landed during the birthing fiasco.

"Do you have muscle relaxants?" She didn't stop moving her hands over him as she talked.

"A beer?" He'd prefer that right now to any pills. He'd seen too many guys sliding into relying on them to get out of bed every day.

"Not the same thing. I don't have anything here."

Her voice trailed off as she slowly, thoroughly and painfully poked at his cheek. "You didn't break anything, but you should have tended to this immediately. We'll get ice for your cheek and back after I check your vitals, then I'll help you to bed. Do you need to use the bathroom?"

He blushed, darn it. No man wanted a woman asking him if he needed help in that department. "I'm good."

"I've been a nurse and an EMT. I've seen it all."

Could be, but he'd had enough humiliation today. He didn't need much in the way of dignity but he wasn't giving this up.

"I'm getting my bag out of the car. Don't move until I'm back to help you."

She went off. He gathered himself to stand, which would be a long, slow, painful process. He was getting that beer. Then he'd get EllaJayne ready for bed so they both could hit the sack. Tomorrow would be bad but he'd have to keep moving. The job only paid well if he showed up, no matter what had happened today.

His arms still worked, thank the Lord, which allowed him to lever himself to a crouched-over stand. He couldn't straighten just yet. He shuffled to the fridge, stopping twice for a cramp to release his leg muscles.

He took two long chugs of beer and toddled with a gait less steady than EllaJayne's toward the bedroom.

"Stop," Pepper said. "You're going to fall." She wedged herself against him. He wished he could appreciate her fragrant softness. She smelled of spicy sausage. His stomach growled despite the pain. He couldn't be too bad if he was hungry.

"Got extra-strength aspirin in my gear."

"That's a good idea. I'll get you settled in bed with ice, then food, then aspirin. No beer." She held onto his bottle and had him moving down the hall before he could say boo.

Fortunately, the bed sat well off the ground and he could fall onto its pillowy top. She tried to strip him, but he fended off her attempts, allowing her to only pull off his boots and socks. She efficiently rolled him onto his stomach, left with the beer bottle and came back with ice packs for his spine and face.

"I'll be back in twenty minutes to move those and you."

Was that a threat or a promise? He'd wanted to say that but hadn't had enough breath. Damn it, he hurt. Just falling onto the bed had put his back into spasms again. By the time he counted to forty-two, the ice had numbed the muscles. How long until she returned to torture him? He closed his eyes and waited for the cold to finish numbing his face.

"Boot, Boot. Come," EllaJayne yelled as the dog's toenails scrabbled on the plank floors of the bedroom.

AJ cracked open his eye and saw his naked toddler and the useless shepherd racing around the room. This would not end well. It never did. He took a second to allow himself to imagine ignoring it. Then he moved his arm to push himself up in bed.

Faye's voice floated into the room. "Children, come." Magically, the dog and little girl raced from the room.

He relaxed back into the bed's downy embrace. Could he be selfish until morning and ask the women to care for EllaJayne? He did allow himself to close his eyes. He'd lay here for another five minutes, tops. Then, he'd get up, get the aspirin and find his girl. He'd give her a final snack, settle her into her bed and read her to sleep if she needed it. He'd need to set a double alarm for the morning. He couldn't be late to the ranch.

"Time to take off the ice." The packets of numbness were whisked away before he could protest or even snatch them back. "I'll work on your back. Then we'll sit you up so you can have dinner, then ice again, then sleep."

He tried to break in, explain that EllaJayne would need him—until Pepper tried to sit him up. Obviously, the numbness wasn't muscle deep.

"Relax. Tensing your muscles only makes it worse. We'll wait ten minutes and ice you again. Will you be okay here on your own while I refill the packs?" By the time she came back he wanted to lie down again. Honestly, it had never been this bad before. Instead of helping him lie flat, she put ice behind his back and on his cheek as she eased him back on the pillow. Then she handed him a mug of soup. It was mainly broth. He didn't care. His finally loosening muscles were making him drowsy.

"Thanks," he managed just as she handed him the aspirin.

"All in a day's work."

"EllaJayne—"

"Faye is taking care of her. She'll sleep in our room tonight. It's no bother. You wouldn't be able to get up if she needed something."

"I'm good."

"I don't think so. I'm the professional. I say tonight, we'll take care of that little girl. You'll be with her all day tomorrow."

"I'll be at work."

"There's no way you can work tomorrow. The swelling in your face should be minimal, but your back is another matter. Turn over again. You need another round of ice."

He resisted. "I don't have a choice here. This is the best job I've found so far. This problem with my back isn't new. I'll be okay in the morning. If I dose myself with aspirin, I'll be good to go. I thank you and Faye for watching Baby Girl so I can get sleep."

The ice packs landed on his back, his face pressed into the pillows. "I'll be back in twenty minutes to take these off. Then I'll help you to the bathroom."

He didn't respond but she would not be helping him. When he heard her and Faye in the kitchen, he pushed the ice off and gathered himself. He could stand. He could walk.

PEPPER WAS OUTSIDE the bathroom door when he opened it. "I told you I'd help you."

"Didn't need help." He held himself in the perfect position where his back only ached. The stabbing pain was gone. He stepped forward and his leg buckled, so he reached out to grab at anything to stop his fall. Pepper's surprisingly strong arm and shoulder propped him up.

"Nope. You didn't need any help. I can see that. Do you want to add severe concussion or a broken limb to the mess you've made of yourself?"

"Slow down." He wrenched the words out. God. He didn't want to admit that standing had been about all he'd been capable of. He pulled in a breath, blew it out and readied himself. He could do this because tomorrow he'd have to be fit enough to do ranch work. "I'm ready now."

The two of them shuffled to his room. She got him into bed without another word. She even worked on his back again. When she replaced the ice packs, she asked, "Which ranch are you working at?"

"Why?" He couldn't imagine she cared.

"I know almost everyone within one hundred and fifty miles of Angel Crossing."

Too tired to argue from the brain-sapping pain, he said, "The Double Cottonwood."

"That's a long drive from here. The staff only come to Angel Crossing once in a while."

"The money is good."

"Of course it is. No one wants to work that far from civilization. Let me make a call."

He pushed himself up and held back a moan as his back clenched. "Who are you going to call?"

"The ranch manager. He and Daddy Gene were friends. I'll explain the situation."

"I'm going to work."

"You're not. Don't worry, though, he'll keep the job open until you're ready to go back day after tomorrow at the earliest."

AJ pushed himself up a little farther, wanting to show her that he could do this. "I'm a bull rider. This is nothing."

"Tell it to someone who'll listen. I'm the medical professional here and I say no." He'd get out of this blasted bed. "Look," she went on, ignoring his struggles. "I've helped him out on more than one occasion. He certainly owes me."

"I didn't ask you to call. I don't—"

"I offered. You're staying in bed tomorrow. I'm calling so you don't get fired."

He wouldn't argue with her anymore. He'd just get up early and sneak out.

"By the way, Daddy Gene taught me how to fix trucks and tractors. I know where the distributor cap is. Or maybe I'll take off the spark plug wires. In case you're thinking of sneaking away. And, right now, I can run a whole lot faster than you."

Her smile of triumph should have irked him. Instead, he wanted to grin at her...well, to say it not so politely, he wanted to grin at her cajones.

Chapter Eight

Mrs. Carmichael, or Grammy Marie as she insisted Pepper and EllaJayne call her, looked so happy to see the little girl. She beamed, showing off perfectly polished false teeth and folds of good living that nearly hid her button-black eyes—something like Oggie's. Over her comfortably plump body, she wore stretch slacks and one of the many sweaters she had that were decorated for each season. The woman looked just like a grandmother should.

AJ had been skeptical when Pepper had suggested Mrs. Carmichael, but over the last two days, Pepper had talked up the older woman's stellar childcare skills. AJ agreed that she was worth a try, but it meant that Pepper had to be the a.m. transportation since Grammy Marie's home was in the opposite direction of AJ's job, which he left for long before dawn. Today was AJ's first day back to work after being off a total of two days. It was also the first day of this new schedule. Pepper would have preferred him to stay at home for at least two more days. His answer had been he'd sleep in his truck so she couldn't tamper with it.

"You and Oggie be good," Pepper said as she hugged EllaJayne. The little girl's eyes widened.

"Peep?" she asked, her lower lip trembling.

"You and Grammy Marie are going to play today." Pepper worked to make her voice chipper and positive. She didn't want the girl to cry.

"Home. Boot."

"Not today. You'll play with Grammy Marie."

"Home," EllaJayne said stubbornly.

"Later. First, you and Grammy Marie and her friends will play, then Daddy will pick you up and you'll go home."

The girl tried to glare like AJ did. Pepper had to keep herself from laughing. Then a sly look came over EllaJayne's round-cheeked face. Uh-oh. Pepper knew that there would be bargaining. How had she already learned that? "Peez. Pity peeze."

"Grammy Marie is very sad you don't want to stay." Pepper tried a new tack and gave a nod to Mrs. Carmichael. The grandmotherly woman smiled.

"Home."

Pepper had run out of ideas. At the ranch, she usually invoked playing with Butch to get EllaJayne to comply. Finally, Grammy Marie spoke, "Come on, EllaJayne, there's a baby doll just waiting for you."

"Baby?"

Grammy Marie held out her hand and EllaJayne toddled away with her. The older woman waved at Pepper, dismissing her. She waited for more wails, cries or an escape attempt. Nothing. Pepper walked to her SUV, wondering why she didn't feel happier that EllaJayne had given in relatively easily. Coffee. That was it. Pepper needed more caffeine, plus the car could use a fill-up. She drove to the nearest station. It was owned by a patient and the gas was a few cents more. She stopped, though, because it just seemed right. She pumped her gas, then went inside to pay and get coffee. Pepper checked her watch. She'd better get a move on. Being late on the doctor-is-in day could get her fired. Dr. Cortez was a great boss that way.

"And I got gas, too," she said to her patient—high blood pressure and dry eyes. Pepper swiped her card when the sale was totaled. It didn't go through. She tried two more times before Mr. McCarthy took the card and tried for her. His gaze wouldn't meet hers.

"Seems there's a problem."

"What?"

"The card is declined."

Pepper stood frozen. "It can't be."

"You're over your limit."

She couldn't be. Could she? Without the grant, she'd been using her credit card for the garden at the ranch as well as to pay the attorney looking at the will. Her bank account wasn't in much better shape. She had enough—barely—to pay for her gas and coffee. She handed over the bank card, trying to not feel embarrassed.

Mr. McCarthy smiled as the sale went through. "Don't worry. Happens to everyone."

She took her receipt and hurried away. What was she going to do?

AT 7 P.M., PEPPER was on her way home and still trying to come up with a plan to find more money. She missed having EllaJayne in the backseat "talking" to Oggie. She needed to remember the little girl was a temporary fixture in her life. She and AJ would be moving on. Daddy Gene had taught Pepper that. Not that he'd moved on, but he'd told her all about watching out for rodeo cowboys. He said he'd stuck around because he'd ridden himself to ground, like they did to unruly stallions. "Just let 'em run till they can't run no more, then run them again. Takes the fight right out of 'em, then the barn looks danged good. That's what I done." She could so clearly hear him and see her mother's knowing smile.

This had nothing to do with the little seed of a fantasy of her, AJ and EllaJayne living at the ranch, growing food and even keeping the spitting llamas. She could see a circle of women making the fleece into yarn and then the beautiful scarves and sweaters they made sold to bring in much-needed money to their families.

Regardless of the lawsuit—which she might have to drop with her credit maxed out—she'd talk with Faye about using the fleece from the Beauties to help the local women. Instead of a quilting bee, they could do a spinning and knitting bee. Pepper could see that as another way for Angel Crossing to help itself. Hadn't she read about a small town somewhere in Arizona or maybe New Mexico setting up an art cooperative? She'd research that and add it to her ever-changing plan. She could already imagine people feeling better about their town, getting healthier with the food from the community gardens and then finding new ways to earn cash. She had become a PA to help people. This was just another way to do that.

"Hello," she called, as she walked to the kitchen. Not a sound. Even Butch was missing, making her worry. Had something happened to EllaJayne? Had

AJ hurt himself again? She went out to the patio. No one. No noises except the brush of a hoof from the Beauties. Then she caught the light in the small barn they used to store weed-killing chemicals and the sharp blades for cutting down brush. She pulled her phone from her pocket, ready to call for help. She didn't know why but a dark weight of disaster had landed on her chest. Her brain ran through all the possible horrors she might see when she walked into the barn.

Filling the middle of the space was Pepper's first greenhouse. Before she could ask any questions, Butch barked and EllaJayne squealed, "Peep." Pepper was not an easy name for a toddler to say.

"Look what we found. You can get back in the growing business," Faye said, her enthusiasm genuine.

AJ didn't turn but stood at the greenhouse, fussing...yes, the big bad sexy cowboy was fussing with the ties that held the plastic in place.

Pepper asked the obvious. "Where did you find this? I thought it'd been thrown away." Then she added because Faye was involved, "Exactly what are you planting?"

"Always so suspicious," Faye said. "It's beans. That's a good crop, right? We were going to do the broccoli next but Butch ate the seeds."

"Boot like bockalee," EllaJayne screeched and hugged the dog, who looked pleased with the world.

"How much did you help, AJ? You didn't overwork your back, did you? Did you eat?"

Finally, he turned and his face was blank. "I just put things together. This was all Faye's idea. We ate."

"What do you think? It will help, right?" Faye asked hopefully.

Her mother might live in a world that paralleled the real one at times, but she really did love her daughter. Pepper never doubted that...or now that she was an adult woman never doubted it. As a teen that had been a different matter. "It'll definitely help. We'll get the seedlings started and then we can transplant them when they're big enough. By then, we should have things plowed and ready. It looks like you're done and I'm starved."

In the bustle of corralling the dog and the child as well as putting away the gardening equipment, Pepper hadn't noticed AJ had wandered off. She couldn't worry about that now. He looked okay and he was fully capable of caring for himself, except...he was a cowboy. Of course, if she hadn't insisted, he would've gone to work even though he could barely move. She needed fuel, then she'd track him down to make sure he hadn't done more damage.

Pepper and EllaJayne sat at the kitchen table while Faye brewed a special tea. The little girl played with her plate full of Oaty O's, stacking them and knocking them down. Pepper didn't even care that Faye had added kimchi to her sandwich, she was so hungry.

Faye turned from her tea and stared at Pepper. "You'll call the attorney tomorrow and tell him that you're done." Her mother didn't smile, didn't show any of her usual compassion.

"The lawsuit isn't just about the garden and my plan. It'll help you, too."

"I don't want it."

"I'm sure Daddy Gene meant to change his will.

He wouldn't have wanted to leave you in such a position."

"I'll be fine."

"Faye," Pepper started. "I loved Daddy Gene. I talked with him a lot, especially after he got so sick, and I know what he wanted."

"He wanted you to be happy. Now, you must call the lawyer tomorrow and tell him you've changed your mind." Faye sat a cup of steaming tea in front of Pepper. "I can see something happened today. You know that's because you're putting negative energy out into the universe with this suit, right?"

"My credit card is over the limit." There was no use not telling Faye because she'd find out eventually. The gossip-vine was too good in Angel Crossing.

Faye went pale and her voice dipped. "Pepper, don't you see you've got to stop fighting the will?"

"'Top," EllaJayne mimicked.

"I'm doing this for Angel Crossing and even for you," Pepper insisted. Her long-range plan was for the ranch to bring in enough from renting lots for an income for Faye.

"It's not. It's for you and your ego." Faye suddenly stiffened, then said with more conviction than Pepper had ever heard, "I won't accept the ranch, and if you keep fighting the will, I'll leave. I'll take my Beauties and go. Dove's Paradise could use the fleece."

Pepper would have laughed off the threat but Faye's core of steel was showing. "It doesn't make—"

"I won't accept it. I should have stopped you sooner."

Pepper stared into her mother's green eyes, so different from her own. The one thing Faye had passed to her was a stubbornness that had gotten them both through a lot. Her mother would walk away if Pepper continued to try to overturn the will. "I'll call the attorney tomorrow," Pepper said, and AJ came into the kitchen.

"What's happened now?" His gaze ping-ponged between the women.

Faye answered, "Pepper is listening to the universe. She's dropping the lawsuit."

"AJ?" Pepper asked as she tapped on the door to his bedroom.

He rushed to stop her from rapping again so Ella-Jayne didn't hear her second favorite person in the world—right behind Butch. "Shh. I just got her down," he said, sidling out. Dang it. He'd closed himself up in his room to stay out of Pepper's way.

They went to the kitchen and she rooted through a cabinet before holding up a bottle of whiskey. "Would you like a drink?"

"Sure."

She poured the liquor and sat with him at the table. After a small sip, she said, "I do actually plan to tell the attorney to drop the suit."

Drinking the entire of bottle couldn't have made him feel any more off kilter. "You will?"

"Not because of Faye and the 'universe.' The lawyer said we didn't have much of a case and…I'm not sure how I'll pay the bill I've already racked up. I'd wanted to talk with you about buying the ranch on a payment plan, but I can't even do that now. So…I've talked with Danny about moving the garden idea onto vacant lots in town, which might work even better.

I'll talk with my patients about finding homes for the Beauties. I can make it work even without Santa Faye Ranch."

"If you do raised beds in town, you should double your yield."

"I thought you were a cowboy."

"I've done some reading." He stared hard at the whiskey. He didn't want to see whatever was in her voice reflected in her eyes.

"You know, Angel Crossing could be on the cutting edge with in-town community gardens. I've been reading more and more that urban farming can be a revitalization technique. There are even gardens in New York City like that. Wouldn't it be great?"

He couldn't resist her enthusiasm. "I saw the article you printed out. Angel Crossing would be lucky to have you helping them to create that. The town. Well, you know what it's like."

"When the mine closed, most of the businesses left. We only got reliable internet access two years ago. We don't even have a full-time doctor."

"My hometown is kind of the same."

They both stared at their glasses, until she finally broke the silence. "The work at Double Cottonwood going okay?"

"Not bad." He wouldn't think about whether he'd be there in another month. If he did a good job, maybe they'd keep him on as a cowhand, at least until the inheritance was settled. *If* it didn't work out, he could go back to the rodeo, except there was EllaJayne and the ranch and—

He'd always been, like his buddy Danny, good at shootin' the breeze with anyone from buckle bunnies to old-timers to fellow competitors. Now words just jammed up in his mouth. Every one either sounded backwoods stupid or more flowery than a Sunday morning TV preacher.

"I guess I'd better—" Pepper said just as he unjammed his tongue to say, "Why don't you show me—" They each laughed in the nervous way of two human beings acting like circling dogs, not sure of the welcome and ready to tuck tail and run.

AJ took the conversational bull by the horns. "I'm all healed up so why don't you show me what you want tilled. It's the least I can do for you, after you took care of my back and EllaJayne. What about manure? You got anything from those yarn balls with four legs? I can work that in. There's some ancient horse manure, too, isn't there? Wish I could have brought Benny with me. But I wasn't sure where I'd land and if there'd be a place for him."

Pepper looked at him with her autumn-brown gaze quickly warmed to something like interest and maybe a tinge of happiness. "I'll get a sweater and meet you at the field."

The unnaturally bright lights on the two barns and the pole by the house illuminated her field and the milling Beauties. Still, shadows made parts of the yard darkly secretive. He wanted to pull her into that shadow and kiss her. Half a year ago, he'd have done that. "This area you have marked off, right?"

They walked around the sections she'd staked off, each a neat rectangle with paths between to make access for weeding and harvest possible.

"I want the folks who'll benefit from the crops to be able to help. Most of them have probably done this at some point in their lives, but we've forgotten where food comes from and how different it tastes when it comes out of the ground and goes right on the table. Plus, I've already tried to get vouchers for food and no one would take them. They don't want a handout. If they put in the work, then they'll get the food. I've already come up with a formula: one hour in the garden equals five pounds of vegetables. Or they can deliver produce."

He never could have imagined he would get hot under the collar listening to a woman talk about how she was helping her neighbors. He'd always said the only woman he wanted was one with long legs and a short fuse. Now, here he was wondering how he could get Pepper into his arms so he could kiss her until she…what?

"Angel Crossing is lucky to have you." He and EllaJayne were lucky, too.

"It's just my job. I can't treat my patients if they don't have the food they need."

"Maybe. But I don't see your doctor doing this."

"He doesn't live here." She stood, feet planted and looking out over the patch of ground. She didn't wear a hat or boots most of the time, but she was more of a cowgirl than any of the women he'd ever known.

"That's not it. You care. You see what needs to be done and you do it." He stepped closer and caught the lemon and clove he'd come to know as Pepper. The hint of her scent made him want to bury his face into the hollow of her collarbone. Right there, he was sure her skin was soft and so fragrant that he'd—

"I've always done what was needed. Faye doesn't always have both feet on the ground."

"Or her taste buds wrapped around real food."

Pepper laughed with her whole body. "I smelled her famous 'Energy Casserole.'"

"Is that what that was? I just closed my eyes, held my nose and hoped for the best."

"When she made that, I always said I'd had a snack and wasn't hungry. Daddy Gene would sneak me banana and peanut butter sandwiches before I went to bed."

"I'm out of Fiddle Faddle, too."

She'd turned and even in the unnatural light, he caught her smile and the transformation of her face. Could he taste that joy? He stepped up to her, lowered his head and pressed his lips softly to her smiling ones before he could think.

"Oh." She breathed out and he didn't resist, slipping his tongue into her tantalizing mouth. He cupped her jaw, his fingers sensitive to the vibrations of pleasure racing along the tender edge. Her own hands rested lightly at his waist, everywhere they touched warmed with sensation.

"Mmm. Better than caramel corn," he whispered against her lips. He pulled her against him slowly, giving her a chance to her to slip away as he hoped and prayed she wouldn't.

Chapter Nine

Pepper should not have been surprised by the hard strength of AJ's shoulders and waist when she'd held on as he kissed her mouth, her neck and then the hollow of her throat. Even now, weeks later, her breath came a little faster. The man might not know much about living in a house of women or even about growing veggies—except what he'd read on the internet—but he did know how to kiss. He hadn't learned that on Kiss.com. Unfortunately, she had a good idea how he'd come by that knowledge. Daddy Gene had warned her that what brains hadn't rattled out of bull riders' skulls settled between their—

"Pretty plants." AJ broke into her thoughts. "Pat them nice, Baby Girl."

Had she come out here again knowing AJ would show up? He and EllaJayne had been spending every evening in the greenhouse. As summer approached, the days were getting longer and she enjoyed checking the garden, weeding and picking off bugs. For some it might have been more work after a long day. But Pepper loved it and she lo—enjoyed AJ and Ella-Jayne coming out to keep her company. Although yesterday the toddler had pulled out half a row of plants before they'd figured out what she'd been up to.

"Peep," EllaJayne said, and Pepper turned to smile at the little girl and motion her closer. Butch was there, too, sniffing between the rows. He might not herd the Beauties but he watched out for EllaJayne.

"See," she said to the little girl, ignoring the man who stood not far away. "Soon it'll have a flower. We won't pick them, right?" EllaJayne shook her head vigorously, her straight fall of hair swinging wildly. Pepper looked up. AJ's own similarly dark hair curled at the sides and in messy tangles along his nape. "You both need haircuts. I'll do it this weekend." She startled herself with her own pronouncement.

"You're a barber, too? You've got no end to talents," AJ said.

"I think I can handle the two of you before you begin to look like you've been living at Dove's Paradise."

"I can return the favor if you want. I was good at trimming up Benny's mane and tail."

"No way. I go to Tucson for a day of beauty every six weeks or so."

"You do it so you can go to Taco Gino's and get a Philly Cheesesteak Chimi."

"Never." She couldn't stop the grin. One night talking in the kitchen about the garden, he'd pried out of her the guiltiest of her pleasures—a hole-in-the-wall taco place in Tucson near the university. Faye would have a fit and cleanse Pepper with a nasty tea or herbal potion if she knew her daughter had eaten a deep-fried tube of steak oozing processed cheese food. She also didn't let her medical professional side tell her how bad the taste-bud nirvana was for her.

"Next time you're taking me," AJ declared.

"We'll see. Maybe. *If* you let me cut your hair and EllaJayne's. I can't be seen hanging out with a shaggy cowboy."

"Otherwise you'd like to be seen with me?"

"Why not? You were a big-time bull rider, right? Isn't that what every cowgirl wants?" She hoped a little snark would add back the distance she'd lost. Why had she said she'd cut his hair? Dear Lord. She'd be so close. She'd be touching him again and again.

"I'm not a bull rider anymore. Just a cowboy with a little girl and a living to earn. Although at the rate I'm going, I'll run out of places to draw a wage before EllaJayne has her next birthday."

"Oh, no. Double Cottonwood is letting you go?"

"I knew it was temporary when I was hired on."

"You want me to ask around?" This conversation was where she wanted to be with him. Friends. Her providing expertise and help, like she did as a PA. Then she would only see him as a patient, like any of the other local men she treated at the clinic.

"If you don't mind," he said and turned away. "Baby Girl, are you petting the plants nice?"

The toddler looked up, her nearly black eyes guileless in her chubby face. "Pretty." EllaJayne patted a plant almost flat.

"Why don't you help me get the straw?" Pepper asked as she walked over and scooped the little girl up. "We'll spread it around to keep down the weeds. We don't want any of those yucky old weeds."

"Yucky weeds," EllaJayne echoed. Pepper didn't

want the intimacy that had been wrapping around her and AJ. The two of them were roommates at best and not for much longer. The court system, now that she wasn't making noises about contesting the will, was slowly grinding forward.

"You two ladies take care of that," AJ shouted. "I'll settle the Beauties."

Pepper smiled. AJ, who'd been less than enthused with the llamas and alpacas, had come to a détente with the little herd. They stampeded Pepper given a chance, and Faye would rather let them roam the desert to find their inner animal. AJ had them disciplined now, and he'd even talked about asking around for someone to take care of their fleeces. He said that they should be able to get decent money for them. He'd done internet research. She wondered how he'd known she'd been planning the same thing.

"Boot," EllaJayne said over Pepper's shoulder, her arm thrust out and waving at her buddy. "Boot." The dog obediently followed them.

Pepper filled the wheelbarrow as Butch and Ella-Jayne solemnly watched, then the girl "helped" Pepper wheel the pile to the rows of beans.

EllaJayne, with Butch's help, scattered more hay than spread, but they stayed entertained. When Pepper finished, she stood with EllaJayne on her hip looking out over her patch of garden and could see, really see, what it could look like if she stayed or if she could afford to buy the ranch. They'd have acres of vegetables and then she'd put in fruit trees and maybe strawberries. Since finding that kind of money was beyond anything she could manage, she'd call the mayor tomorrow about the empty lots in town.

She could transform those into gardens that would provide the same sort of produce she'd imagined at Santa Faye Ranch. Or maybe she should approach AJ with something she'd thought about. A rent-to-own situation. She'd pay him so much per month to stay on the ranch. The trouble was the amount she could afford per installment. She'd put that idea on the far-back burner.

"Peep," EllaJayne said sleepily before her head thunked down on Pepper's shoulder. Darn it. The little one's bedtime had come and gone. AJ must still be dealing with the Beauties. While she and Faye often helped entertain EllaJayne in the evenings, AJ always put her to bed and usually stayed in the room, watching the small TV he'd found with a pile of trash. It worked, he said, and was the best price: free.

She'd take EllaJayne inside and get her ready for bed while he wrangled the herd. She could do this for them. Since he was caring for the Beauties, it was only fair.

PEPPER LAY ON the couch watching TV with a sweet-smelling and sleeping EllaJayne stretched across her chest. Her own eyes drooped, and she wondered how much longer she should wait for AJ to make his way inside. She didn't feel right about entering their bedroom anymore to lay the little girl down. He had another fifteen minutes, then she would go out to look for him. She set her internal clock and closed her eyes, confident that she'd wake up. She always did, a trick she'd learned as a kid.

"Pepper," said a deep voice. "I'll take EllaJayne."

She cracked open her eyes. AJ's face was on level with hers. She started back. "What?"

"Whoa." His hand shot out and covered hers where it lay on the girl's back. "Didn't mean to startle you."

His rough-palmed hand fit easily over top of Pepper's. "What time is it? Where were you?" Pepper struggled to sit up and AJ let go of her. EllaJayne whined and wriggled. Pepper stopped, not wanting to wake her.

AJ's voice fell to a soft whisper. "One of those cotton balls got out. It took time to get her back with the others. I know I need to get EllaJayne to bed but could you watch her for another ten minutes? I want to get cleaned up."

Pepper nodded. She watched his cowboy swagger, not taking her eyes from him for medical reasons only. After all, she had to check to make sure his back problem hadn't flared up again. Clinical interest. That's all she had.

EllaJayne had fallen back into a limp-limbed sleep, so Pepper carefully sat up, ready to stop if she made any movement. She nuzzled a little closer. Pepper stared at the TV, wondering when the smell of baby powder had gotten so soothing. That was dangerous, though. EllaJayne wasn't hers and neither was her daddy. Both of them were visitors in her life. AJ had made clear that as soon as he could sell the ranch, he would. Maybe she shouldn't give up on the idea of buying it. There had to be a grant or an organization that would help. Her plan had so much—

"I can take her now." AJ reappeared and leaned close. Pepper pulled away instinctively, then relaxed her shoulders so she could lift the girl away and toward AJ.

"Here she is." Pepper released EllaJayne to her daddy and immediately wanted her sleep-warm weight back.

"Thanks." AJ didn't move. Pepper looked at him, the muscles of his arms bunching and shifting as he adjusted the little girl onto his shoulder. She stood, abruptly wanting…needing to be far away from him. She was not the kind of woman who went for cowboys, especially of the rodeo variety.

Pepper kept her voice level. "I'll ask around about work." AJ nodded and she got up and slipped past him without touching. Faye had taught her to respect her body's needs. Not this time. AJ would be as bad for her as a Philly Cheesesteak Chimi.

AJ WATCHED THE dark strands of his daughter's hair slide to the kitchen floor with every snip of Pepper's scissors. He couldn't decide if he liked the way it made her look less like a baby and more like a little girl. Dear Lord. He had a daughter who'd date cowboys. He reminded himself that was years from now. He would be better at this daddy thing by then. He'd better be, because right now his skills were only marginally better than his own parents'.

"Boot," EllaJayne squealed pulling away from Pepper and reaching toward the dog.

"Darn it," Pepper said.

"What?" he asked as his eyes scanned over his daughter, looking for blood.

"Her bangs. I'm so sorry. She moved just as I was doing the center."

His daughter's bangs were not a nice even line. A

large chunk was missing from the middle of the dark fringe of hair. He laughed.

Pepper stared at him, her face starting to relax. "I really am sorry."

"It's hair. It'll grow back. I think we're done. Maybe later you can try to even it out." He had to raise his voice as EllaJayne squirmed and screeched for the dog. Pepper nodded and quickly swept off the towel they'd used to keep hair out of her clothes. He lifted her from the chair and put her on the ground with Butch. The two of them immediately ran around the table, scattering hair.

"Out. AJ, get them out," Pepper said. He lifted his now-kicking daughter and carried her back to the bathroom for her nighttime scrub down. Less than thirty minutes later, his Baby Girl and Butch were asleep. He'd tried to chase Butch from the bedroom. The dog wouldn't budge. He could have carried him out, but it hadn't seemed worth the effort. Today had been another long one. He wasn't complaining, though. It was work. If he was lucky, he'd have another week, maybe two. So far Pepper hadn't turned up any leads, and he hadn't either, at least not anything in reasonable driving distance. Going back to the rodeo was beginning to look more like a certainty.

"Your turn," Pepper said, pointing him to the makeshift barber chair as he stood in the kitchen's archway.

"You don't need to do me."

Pepper grinned. "Good to know, but I was just going to cut your hair. Ever consider a beard to go with the mountain man look?"

"In the winter in Kentucky, I had one…sometimes.

Keeps your face warm when you go out to take care of animals."

"Scarves do the same thing."

He grunted because he really didn't want to talk about Kentucky. He had an idea that having her cut his hair wasn't a good idea and not because of the missing chunk in his daughter's bangs.

"Over to the sink," Pepper said. "I can't cut that mop when it's dry. Sit on the stool there. You can lay back in the sink. Just like a salon."

He hesitated. Now, wasn't this a kick in the head. He was scared. Afraid of Pepper and her nearness. Ridiculous. He could do this. She'd trim up his hair, probably a good thing since he was on the hunt for a new job. He sat and leaned back.

Water ran in the sink and then Pepper leaned over him and her breast brushed his shoulder. How could he not have anticipated what would happen? He was a bull rider, he should have been able to predict the next corkscrew twist. Pepper shifted and her breast moved as she reached over him. Now, she was nearly pressed chest to chest with him. Was she doing that deliberately?

"Hope you don't mind baby shampoo," she said as her fingers dug into his scalp, massaging in the soap.

He waited for his leg to start twitching like Butch's did when AJ found the perfect place to scratch. When her fingers found a spot at his nape, he moaned.

"Did I hurt you?" Pepper asked and her fingers stilled.

He stifled another moan. He didn't want her to stop. The pleasure-pain of her massage had released the tension all over his body. "No," he said, his voice hoarse. "You a professional?"

"We lived without a shower or tub for a while." Her fingers went back to their magic work and every one of his muscles melted, just like butter on a stack of pancakes. Behind his closed lids, the stack of pancakes disappeared and instead he saw Pepper leaning over him, her lovely pink-as-a-carnation lips soft and ready—

"All done," said the real Pepper.

He cracked open his eyes, giving himself a few seconds to gather what was left of his wits. He stood, staying hunched to hide the part of him behind his zipper that had been obviously paying attention and shuffled to the chair. His body hummed with the touch of her fingers, her breasts and the scent of her skin.

"You want me to go short or just trim it up?"

She distracted him from the words with her fingers moving through the wet strands and skimming along his skull. He turned his moan into a hum of agreement.

"Okey dokey, then." The scissors snipped close to his ear, jerking him from his pleasurable haze. "Careful. I don't want to nick you."

He stilled. "I don't need anything fancy."

"Don't worry. You won't get anything fancy. This is strictly an I-don't-want-to-go-to-the-barbershop cut."

"I didn't know there was such a thing."

"I gave Daddy Gene that kind of cut a lot. Faye, too. Now, be quiet and I'll get this done."

He shut up and closed his eyes. He didn't want to

have his vision filled with her chest because then he could imagine—nothing. He didn't have a towel or anything else to hide his interest if he let his thoughts run wild, like Pepper in the cowgirl seat above him, naked, sweaty and ready—

"Did you say something?" Pepper with the scissors asked. He needed to remember that Pepper.

"Just, umm…" He shifted in the seat to distract himself.

"Watch it. You're wrigglier than EllaJayne." Her hand squeezed his shoulder. That touch shuddered through him. She stilled. "I see that…well, okay—"

His hand reached up and lay over hers. She didn't pull away. He picked up the magical hand and kissed the palm. He heard her intake of breath and rubbed his nose into her wrist, a place soft and fragrant with shampoo and the fresh lemon that clung to her. The rich scent made him imagine darkened rooms. He kissed her wrist, her forearm, then she was in his lap and her mouth was on his, the carnation pink lips as soft as he remembered.

He didn't start the kiss softly. He couldn't. A storm had started low in his gut. His mouth devoured hers as she opened to him, her fingers finding that magical spot at his nape. He pulled her closer but not close enough. He stood, lifting her easily, and her mouth nuzzled into the space at the top of his open shirt. He had to have her laid out where he could taste and touch. Not his bedroom and not hers. She stilled. He knew that he had to move. He couldn't let the spell of heat and sex blow away. Not now. He rushed out to the patio and the lounge with its thick cushion. He got her settled with another long kiss, the chair just big enough for the two of them—if they stayed close. He threw his leg over her hip. Through their clothes, her yearning heat warmed him from chest to groin. Closer. He needed to be closer. He didn't even know he'd said that out loud until Pepper answered, "Yes," as her hands worked at all his buttons at once.

His own hands yanked at her jeans and her shirt until he met her buttery soft skin. Taste. He had to taste. Half-dressed he slipped from the lounge so he could bury his mouth into the softness of her belly and then upward to her straining breasts. Her hands clutched at the back of his head.

"Arthur John, you are a devil," she moaned out as she arched under his lips, tongue and teeth.

"Then you're a witch," he whispered, laying himself out on top of her so he could return to her sweet carnation mouth. She opened to him, her legs wrapping around him, holding him tight to her so that their bodies aligned. So that there was no question what they each wanted.

Chapter Ten

Pepper's breath caught again in her throat as AJ's hands and mouth made love to her. Sweetly, hotly and with expertise. She gasped over and over. Except it wasn't enough. She wanted them skin to skin, nothing between them.

"Pepper, honey," he whispered into her ear, his slow Kentucky drawl thick and dark, like molasses and whiskey. "I can't wait. I need you now, darlin'."

He didn't move though and she wanted him to, like she'd never wanted another man. "Why are you talking?"

"I need you to be sure," he said, hushed and serious. His lips at the lobe of her ear as his words brushed along her face.

"I'm sure. I want you, now, AJ McCreary, and if you don't—"

He moved enough that together they quickly stripped her of her shirt and pants. He slowed her hands on the clasp of her bra, watching with wide eyes as it came off, while he slid his hands under her panties and pulled down. His fingers drifted over her before he turned away for a condom packet, then he was back to her ready, eager, but so in control she wanted to scream.

"If I do anything you don't like, you just tell me, ya hear."

She held his face as he braced himself above her, and she shivered in delight at the moon-silvered strength of him. "I'm a woman, not a girl. I will always tell you what I 'like.' Right now, I'd like you to stop stalling." A devilish smile to match his pirate-dark hair made her vibrate with anticipation. Then she no longer thought but only felt his heat and hers building and building until she cried out.

He whispered in a hoarse voice, "Let's see if we can't make you 'like' it again."

PEPPER COULDN'T READ the stars to know what time it was or how long they'd been spooned together on the narrow lounge. She enjoyed the press of their flesh. Neither of them had said a single word since they'd used the last of AJ's condoms. Not that he had a huge stack. The haze was lifting, and Pepper's brain was re-engaging. She refused to regret what she'd done, but she knew it needed to be a one-of.

"Boot!" a crackling, amplified little-girl voice broke the silence. Pepper jerked.

AJ jumped from the lounge, impressively and explosively fast as he went to his jeans. EllaJayne called the name one more time, then silence. He pulled on his clothes. With his back to her, in what Pepper assumed was a gentlemanly way to allow her to dress in privacy, he finally said, "The new baby monitor has an app for my phone."

"Oh," Pepper said, looking for her socks, after pulling her top over her head. "That's convenient."

"Much better than carrying around the walkie-talkie thingy."

So this was the way it was going to be. They'd pretend that what had happened hadn't? "Sounds like she went back to sleep."

"She does that. She talks a lot. At least she doesn't go sleep-walking. Had an uncle who did that."

They were both dressed and facing each other. Pepper kept her gaze somewhere over his right shoulder. Even though the now shadowed darkness of the patio wouldn't have let him see her face, she didn't want to take the chance, not sure what she feared exactly.

"Somnambulism can be a problem and a sign of sleep apnea or even heart trouble."

"Huh."

She interpreted that as a marginally interested noise. He stepped toward the house and froze, going stiff before taking another careful step. "Stop. Did you hurt your back again?" She went to his side, her hand tracing over his lower spine to feel what was going on. He skidded from her touch. "Did that hurt?" What had their… Had they damaged his back somehow?

"I'm fine. I don't need you poking at me."

"I could see your back is giving you trouble." She used her firm clinic voice.

"I'm not a flippin' patient." His words came out on a rush of air as his gaze kept steady on her face.

She pulled back immediately. "I'm sorry. I just saw your back hurt and—"

"Jeez. What man wants to…after we…jeez. I'm a
g.d. guy. Give me a little dignity, okay? I want you
to at least remember what I…jeez." He rubbed at his
neck. "I'd rather face Tornado," he mumbled.

Lordy be. Men could be so dumb. Or maybe not.
Would she want him to treat her like something less
than a woman after what they had just done? On im-
pulse she stepped up and pulled his head down for a
kiss. His arms wrapped around her, and he stepped
into the lip-lock that caused explosions through her
body. How could she want more? But she did. That
one thought had her pulling away slowly…but still
moving away. "I know you're all man, sweetie." She
gave him what she hoped was a saucy smile. The
trembling wasn't in her lady parts. It was her heart,
scaring and exciting her at the same time.

AJ DIDN'T GRAB Pepper again, even though that was
what he wanted to do. Bad idea. The two of them had
just had amazing…sex. He had to remember that's
all it was. She'd tried to take his ranch. She'd made it
clear she thought rodeo cowboys were only one small
step up from puppy kickers. Plus, he had his daughter
to think about. He'd be selling out and moving on.
California might still work out. He'd always wanted
to live where the sun shone every day. Arizona had
that, an annoying voice said, and what about asking
Pepper if she was interested in paying him to use the
property for the garden, once she reimbursed her attorney? That was a pipe dream.

The lingering scent of clove and lemon snapped him
from his thoughts. They'd had a damned…moment.
Yep. That's what it was. A little craziness for both of

them but no reason to change any plans. He stepped toward the house and stopped as pain shot down into his hip again. Taking a deep breath, he looked into the house. The kitchen was empty. He could get a beer and an aspirin. The two would settle his back and his mind. He had to be up early—as always. He also needed to be using his time and energy on finding a new job. He was already behind on his truck payment and his daughter needed new clothes. She'd outgrown nearly everything she'd had when they'd landed at Santa Faye Ranch more than two months ago.

As he sipped his beer in the bedroom, he ran through what he'd need to do the next day, and it overwhelmed him. He already knew the next evening, Pepper wouldn't be waiting for him in the garden, ready to talk about their days, figure out their schedules and just hang while they did the relaxing work of caring for the fields and animals.

Darn it. He knew sex messed things up. Maybe not this time? He snorted. Sex would more than mess it up this time. Pepper wasn't a buckle bunny or a woman looking for a honky-tonk good time. She was a woman who cared—deeply—and wouldn't take what they'd done lightly. What he wanted to do again and what he deep-in-his-gut feared would be difficult to forget.

AJ HATED BEING RIGHT. Their night…not even a night… on the lounge a week ago had messed with whatever had been happening between him and Pepper. If he accidentally brushed up against her now, she jumped away like she'd touched a boiling pot. He hadn't known how much he'd liked those casual touches and how much he'd miss the evenings in the field together with EllaJayne. It was all wrecked now.

"Yeah, sorry about that, son," he said out loud to the face in the mirror as he shaved. Baby Girl yelled for Boot from the floor of the bathroom. He'd had to give up on her car seat as a corral. She'd figured out the extra tie he'd put over the buckle she'd Houdini-ed her way out of when he'd been under the hood on that first day in Angel Crossing. He tried to keep her in his peripheral vision because she'd figure out the bathroom lock soon enough, then she'd roam freely. She made a pitiful cry for Butch again. Another five minutes and she could be reunited with the useless dog. Yesterday while AJ had been moving the Beauties, Butch had raced through the herd, scattering them. Two hours later, AJ had finished rounding them up—with Butch locked away in the house. Good thing the llamas and alpacas had a weakness for black licorice.

Now, his daughter happily played with her toes, then picked up Oggie, talking to the flattened toy. "What am I going to do?" he asked her. She stopped chattering and held out the dog to him. A big compliment. "Thank you, honey. You keep Oggie." When had he gotten so soft that tears sprang into his eyes because his daughter offered him her darned toy?

Since he was facing the fact he might just have to leave her.

He'd looked everywhere for work. Everywhere that paid a decent wage with decent hours. Then, of course, the rodeo had come a-callin'. One stock contractor he'd worked for was looking for a replacement wrangler and was willing to pay top dollar. It meant AJ would need to hit the road. It would mean…what?

Could he take Baby Girl? Yeah, right. Exactly how would that work? He could leave her here, couldn't he? EllaJayne liked the Bourne women much better than she did him most days. After all, he was the one who made her go to *b-e-d*.

Leaving Baby Girl wasn't forever, not like her mama had. It was just until he could get caught up on the truck payments and other bills. Until the ranch was his. Bobby Ames kept saying it wouldn't be much longer, but that man's idea of long and AJ's weren't exactly the same.

"I'm going to have to do it, EllaJayne. I'll miss you," he choked out. He stared at his face in the mirror again, hardening everything like he did before a ride. He wouldn't think about the possible pain. He'd focus on what he had to do to make it through the next eight seconds. He'd track Pepper down and sweet-talk her into listening to his plan. If that didn't work, could he ask Faye to convince Pepper to care for the little girl with Grammy Marie's help? Faye more often than not acted like a flake but she was more together than her gypsy skirts and herbal remedies had led him and everyone else to believe. He'd begun to understand what Gene had seen in the woman, and how she'd helped raise a daughter like Pepper. The two of them were caregivers, just from different roads. As he'd hoped…sort of…Pepper was in the kitchen finishing up her breakfast when he and EllaJayne were done with their morning bathroom routine. Now what should he do?

"Good morning, EllaJayne. How is Oggie today?" Pepper asked his daughter. The girl squealed in delight.

"I need to talk with you," AJ said. Pepper's eyes widened, before shifting to the doorway. "It won't take long."

She looked down at his daughter who had raced over to sit at her feet, talking again with Oggie. "She needs her breakfast."

"I can take care of that while we talk." He went to the fridge, stopping to get himself a cup of coffee. He needed the shot of caffeine. He plopped his daughter down in her chair.

"Here's the thing," he said as he helped her spoon yogurt into her mouth. "I've been looking for work."

Pepper nodded, standing as far away from him as the kitchen would allow. Dang. She looked cute in her oversize shirt and ratty shorts that she'd obviously slept in. He didn't want to think about her, warm and soft in the morning light in a big bed with nothing on but—"There isn't anything around here. I've looked."

"I thought Danny had leads for you. I can try again with people I know."

He started on his daughter's cereal, focusing on each spoonful. "I've run out of time and my old boss called. I'm going back on the road with the rodeo. For two months, maybe a little longer. I'll make more there than I could anywhere here."

"What are you thinking? You have a daughter."

"I know I have a daughter. That's why I'm doing this."

"You'll drag her with you and leave her with strangers?" Pepper turned away.

"I'm not—" He cleared his throat. How could he leave his daughter if he couldn't even say the words? He would because without the work, neither of them would be okay. "That's why I needed to speak with you. I'm hoping I can count on you…and Faye to look after EllaJayne."

"Look after her? She's not a puppy. Plus, we're talking months. I know I've dropped her off at Grammy Marie's but that's not the same as being solely responsible…that's a lot to ask."

"I know it is, but it's temporary, and I'll get home as often as I can. We should be in Vegas or nearby for part of the time."

"You're telling me there's nothing that you could find—"

"It's not just the wrangling, though that pays well. My boss said he'd stake me for rides. If I end up in the money, I'll be back sooner, rather than later."

"What?" she shouted. "You're going to crawl onto the back of a bull with your…knowing that your daughter… No. I won't do it."

"What do you mean no?" What had he seen before she turned from him again? Fear? Anger?

"I would think even your addled brains could figure that out. *N-O.* I'm not doing it."

"Peep?" EllaJayne asked in a quavering voice, reaching out her hands.

Pepper dashed across the kitchen and snatched up his daughter, obviously forgetting for a moment about the belt that held the little girl in place. AJ fumbled with the buckle along with Pepper's hands. She was close enough for him to see the fear in her usually warm brown gaze.

"It'll be fine," he said gently, like he would to a skittish horse. "It's what I've done for most of my life."

"And look what it's done to you? Your back? Your hip? Do you want to be in a wheelchair? Do you want to have surgery after surgery?" She had Baby Girl in her arms now and buried her face in that sweet baby-smelling spot in the crook of EllaJayne's neck.

"First, that ain't happenin'," he said with the bravado he needed to get through the next few months. "Second, it won't be for long."

"As your…your medical professional, I'm saying you're not fit."

"I can give you money to care for EllaJayne. I wouldn't expect you to do it for free. You could use the money for the garden." His hope had been she'd offer to watch the little girl and not expect cash, but if he had to pay for her as well as Grammy Marie, he would. It wasn't a perfect solution, but it could work until the ranch was his.

"What's wrong?" Faye asked, startling him. AJ hadn't heard her come into the kitchen, his focus on Pepper.

Pepper answered for him. "He's being a cowboy. He wants to go back to the rodeo and expects us to be good little women and watch his child."

"Oh," Faye said. "He's a Taurus."

As usual, exactly what Faye meant eluded him, but he thought she was supporting his decision. "I can't find work locally and I've got bills." That really was it in a nutshell. "I might even have a chance at a few purses. It wouldn't be for long. I told Pepper I'd get back here as often as I can."

"And you need us to watch out for the precious little one? Of course we will. That's what we do for family."

"Family?" Pepper spat out. "He's not family. He's the kind of cowboy Daddy Gene—"

"That's not true," Faye said. "Gene loved Arthur John. Why else would he leave him the ranch? Although maybe he had a bigger plan in mind, but that's not for now. We have a chance to have this wonderful soul all to ourselves. What a great time we'll have. Arthur John has to do this."

"Thanks, Faye." He still needed Pepper to agree. He trusted her—when had that happened? Over the two months they'd been here, it had crept up on him. Or maybe it was that night on the lounge? How could he not trust a woman he'd been…well, been with. "Pepper, what do you say? It'll be best for everyone."

"Except you," she muttered and glared at Faye and him.

"Outside," Faye said, pushing them out the back door and onto the patio. "I'll get EllaJayne ready for her glorious day."

The snick of the lock on the back door worried AJ but not as much as what Pepper wanted to do to his plan.

"I'm a PA. I know what you've done to your body and what more rides could do to it."

She'd come out swinging. He would've admired that tenacity if it hadn't been aimed at him. "It's my body and my decision."

"I'm your doctor."

"You're not and even if you were, I'd still be going out. I've got bills and—" He wouldn't go into the pile of debts he had, having to do with his own misspent youth, paying off EllaJayne's kin. And of course there was his truck and care for Benny back in Kentucky.

"We've all got bills. But you've also got a little girl."

He stepped up to her, wanting to make her understand he had no choice. He was down to the best of the bad choices. "Pepper." He put his hand gently on her arm. Mistake. Big Mistake. "Pepper, I have to." He pulled her into an embrace, speaking softly into her hair. "Honey, I've got to do this. There's no other way until I can sell the ranch." For a second, such a brief moment, she relaxed into him and her arms reached around him. He leaned back enough to take her chin, gave her a chance to pull away, then kissed her. Kissed her for the weeks, months he wouldn't be around to see her, touch her and be with her. Oh, God, she was so spicy sweet. How could he leave her? Sheep tails!

Chapter Eleven

Pepper pulled AJ even closer as his mouth explored hers gently, insistently. The shift of muscle under his shirt took her right back to the lounge. Him. Over her, under her. No. She pulled away, and it felt like tearing a bandage off a wound. He could…would hurt her so badly if she allowed it.

She stepped farther away, feeling the loss of his warmth even under the morning sun that was quickly heating up the patio. She made sure her gaze didn't land on the lounge.

His hand went to his nape and rubbed hard. "I've got to go. I've got no choice. All I need from you is to watch over EllaJayne. If you won't…then I'll take her along. I'll figure something out. I always do."

So he'd use blackmail? He knew she wouldn't allow him to drag that baby over hill and dale, staying with who knew who. The man didn't have the sense God gave…a…a damned llama. "You're fighting dirty and you know it." His jaw tightened and his eyes darkened to rainstorm-gray. Good. He knew she knew what he was doing. "I can't let you bring that toddler on the road. I'll take care of her." She straightened her shoulders because she wouldn't be walked over. "But I have rules."

"Of course you do."

She ignored the snide tone. She needed these concessions. "You will call every day to speak with Ella-Jayne. You'll give me a schedule of when you expect to visit the ranch. Finally, I must be listed on any forms as your emergency contact and as the person medical information can be released to."

"Why would I do that?"

"Because I want to make sure you're okay for Ella-Jayne." Yep, that and he was a patient.

"That's it? I do that and you'll look after her, you and Faye and Grammy Marie?"

What was she agreeing to? To do what had to be done. He was going no matter what she said. She'd come to care for EllaJayne. Her decision was the only one that made sense. "We'll do it as long as you agree to my conditions. When do you leave?" She needed to stay all business and not think about ending up back in his arms.

"Ten days. I'll catch up with Dave in New Mexico." He stood on the patio looking…she didn't know exactly like what, except she had to turn away to keep herself from kissing him again, telling him he shouldn't go and that she'd miss him.

Before her brain fully engaged and made her shut up, she said, "It would take me a little time—I need to pay off my attorney and some other bills—but remember me saying that I could pay you for the house and some acreage over time, like rent to own? You'd still have plenty of land to sell and you'd be getting money while you waited for a buyer. What would be left is better for running cattle anyway." It was the land Daddy Gene had rented out to the next ranch, until they'd closed up shop.

He shook his head and rubbed his nape again. "I can't wait. It's for EllaJayne," he said, raking his fingers through his hair.

The night she'd played barber came back to her, in every nerve ending. Focus on EllaJayne. "It won't be that long, and you might even end up with more money."

"You don't get it. Faye acts like…well, Faye, but she loves you like any other mama. She would never abandon you."

Pepper couldn't understand exactly where the conversation was headed now. She stayed quiet.

"You know that EllaJayne's mama allowed her to go to foster care," he said and paced away from Pepper, hands clenched at his sides. "A little baby. She just dumped her. I don't know why…it doesn't matter why or why she didn't tell me I had a daughter. When I agreed to take Baby Girl…there was paperwork and Suzy, EllaJayne's mama, said she wanted money. For enough cash, she agreed to sign away her rights, that EllaJayne would be all mine. The next payment is due and if I default, Baby Girl goes back to Suzy, which means she'll end up who knows where until I can get to court and prove I'm the daddy and sue for full custody."

Dear Lord, that poor little girl. And AJ. What a burden. She'd made it worse with her insistence on fighting the will, drawing out the settling of the estate. Why hadn't he said anything before? Maybe because she'd been such a pain in his behind. Right now, she needed to act like the adult she was. "AJ," she said as she approached him. "I had no idea. Of course you've got to get the money. If I had any, I would give it to you."

He turned, his eyes so dark with pain and fear, her heart stopped for a second. "I know you would. That's the only reason I feel right about leaving EllaJayne."

Pepper didn't know why but that simple statement made her chest tighten. He trusted her. Really trusted her. Not because she had letters after her name or because it made things convenient for him, but for her, for what she'd said and done. She took his hand, calloused and rough, but so solidly male and dependable. He might be a rootless bull rider, but he did what he could to protect those he loved. He hadn't walked away from his daughter. He stepped in and stepped up.

"Thank you," she said to him as she gave his hand, the one that had touched her so gently, a squeeze. "I... just thank you for trusting me with your daughter. We care about her and want her to be safe and happy."

"That's all I want. Just that. It's not too much to ask, is it? But the darned universe wants to mess it all up." He squeezed her hand back as the frustration made his voice deeper and cloudier.

"You know what Daddy Gene used to say? The universe can go take a flying leap." He stared at her. "He usually said that to Faye."

"Sounds like Gene. What do you think he'd say about the situation now?"

Talking about Daddy Gene didn't hurt so much with him. "He'd say 'Pepper-dew, a cowboy's gotta do what a cowboy's gotta do.'"

"What does that even mean?" His eyes cleared a little, but he didn't drop her hand. Her gaze stayed on him, taking in the soft curve of his lips, the straight shoulders and suntanned skin.

"How would I know? I'm not a cowboy." She smiled when she saw his lips curve and his shoulders relax.

"If I could stay, I would." AJ gripped her hand and his mouth straightened into a firm line.

"I know. Maybe you really aren't a cowboy. Aren't you supposed to be a tumblin' tumbleweed?"

"Not Kentucky cowboys. We're the kind who stick around."

What was he saying? She searched his face, his eyes…something flashed there right before he lowered his head and took her mouth with his. How could this feel so right when he was leaving, no matter what he said about Kentucky cowboys. His arm wrapped around her and pulled her flush to him. She couldn't stop herself from stroking the rigid nape of his neck with her free hand, massaging at the tightness and the vibrating strength of him. She lifted herself onto her toes to put her mouth more solidly on his. He hummed his approval just before unsealing her lips to taste her fully, to make her understand exactly what a cowboy had to do.

When the patio came back into focus, Pepper's hands held onto his arms not sure whether she wanted him closer or farther away. The kiss had been unexpected. She had to be honest with herself, though. It hadn't been unwanted. What did she want, then? Hell. She wanted AJ, a rodeo cowboy with a baby, a debt and more integrity than sense, to be *her* cowboy.

FOR THE WEEK since AJ had told Pepper he'd be hitting
the road, he'd been preparing himself and EllaJayne.
That hadn't been as odd or as difficult as dealing with
the population of Angel Crossing. When he'd gone to
town to pick up this and that at the small, convenience
home-improvement-feed store, he'd gotten unsolicited
advice that all suggested he'd better keep his zipper
up and locked while on the road. Grammy Marie had
been the bluntest. She'd said: "AJ, you know we all
know how to skin a rabbit and shoot a buck. Don't
make us test out our aim and sharpen our knives."

Even Faye had said something about his trip. Her
warning was cloaked in astrological signs, but he'd
known what she meant: keep it in his jeans.

He'd wanted to confront Pepper to find out what
she'd been saying to their neighbors, but his house-
mate had been coming in late and leaving early. She
might be avoiding him. He was leaving day after tomorrow and the final errands and chores would fill
up all those hours.

Today he and Danny were having lunch at the
town's one sad diner. AJ pushed his way into the
Devil's Food. The red-vinyl-topped chrome stools at
the long Formica counter were full and the booths
with the same red vinyl seats and worn tabletops were
mostly occupied. The diners' choices leaned toward
coffee and pie.

He saw Danny in a far booth and two oldsters
standing and wagging fingers at him. This place was
just like Pinetown without the pine trees and slag
heaps. The one diner in his hometown was always on
the edge of killing patrons with the sameness of the
fare and filled with seniors with more opinions than

sense. Danny looked relieved when AJ walked up and slid into the booth. The couple were one of those weather-beaten twosomes whose clothing, while not matching exactly, looked alike. AJ smiled at them.

"Don't grin like an idiot," the woman said. "You're leaving Pepper with your baby."

The man chimed in before AJ could gather his wits. "Marie said she's been watching the little one and you seemed like an okay daddy. Now you're just up and running off."

AJ tried to figure out if there was a question in there. "I've got a job with the rodeo."

The two shook their heads. "Heard that," the woman said. "Just like Gene when he first came to town. Think you can be a family man and chase around the country."

"No, ma'am," AJ said. "Just trying to make a little money until I—"

"Thanks, Loretta," Danny broke in. "I appreciate that you and Irvin are only looking out for the little girl. I'll keep an eye on the situation. AJ and I go way back."

The couple glared hard at AJ before making their goodbyes.

"Don't worry," Danny said. "It's just the Angel Crossing grapevine. Not much goes on, so whatever happens at the clinic or anywhere else in town gets passed around quickly. Marie might be a good kid sitter, but she likes to visit with friends here in the back room and I'm sure you and your daughter have been a hot topic."

"I thought Pinetown was bad. It's got nothing on this."

"We're tight. Have to be so far from much of anything, even the Angel Crossing community college campus is a thirty-minute drive."

AJ decided to move the conversation along. "What should I order?"

"So you've heard about the diner. It's fine. Whatever problems they had were months ago. A bad cook. There's a new one and he's getting things ship-shape. I'm going to have the Cowboy Casserole, nice spicy chili and corn chips with plenty of cheese. Can't go wrong with that combo."

"Sounds good."

"So what do you need from me?"

"Why would you think I need something?"

"Other than that one drink, I haven't heard from you."

"Been busy." Danny's gaze called BS on that comment. "Things have gotten complicated."

"What I heard. So you're getting extra friendly with our Pepper? Damn it, AJ."

"No one's business."

"This is Angel Crossing. It's everyone's business."

"So everyone's concerned now, huh?"

"It's not just Pepper but that little girl of yours Marie dotes on."

"Good thing, then, that I'm talking with the mayor about looking after all of them."

"What do you mean 'looking after all of them'?" Danny's normally smiling face darkened into a frown.

"Run out to the ranch a few times a week to help with the Beauties—"

"Beauties?"

A woman's voice cut in, "So, mayor, what you up

to now? Getting a beauty pageant started? I'll sign up for that."

"Marlena, that just wouldn't be fair." Danny grinned at the frizzle-haired waitress, who wore blue jeans hacked off at the knee and a plaid cowgirl shirt that had had scissors taken to its sleeves, too. Her lined face fell comfortably into a grin.

"You got that right. Now, whadya have?" She took their order and poked fun at Danny, glared at AJ before insulting another customer on her way behind the counter where she pushed their order through a long rectangular window that gave a glimpse into the kitchen.

"Back to these Beauties," Danny said.

"Faye's alpacas and llamas. They don't need a lot of work and Pepper will help if she has the time. And speaking of the lady, her garden will need work, too. She takes care of the weeding and such. I usually haul out the fertilizer, otherwise known as manure, and move the irrigation and portable greenhouses. She has a list. She's really good at those."

"So you're a farmer now."

"I live on Santa Faye Ranch. I help out where I can."

"Uh-huh."

"It's what a normal human being does." Danny was really starting to annoy him. "Finally, I need to ask you to be backup transport for EllaJayne. She'll still be going to Grammy Marie's, but sometimes Pepper can't pick her up or drop her off, and you know Faye can't drive."

"What do you mean she can't drive? Everybody drives."

"Not Faye. She talked about putting a baby seat on her bicycle. We talked her out of that. Maybe with Gene…gone and Pepper so busy, she'll reconsider learning to drive. So…Pepper or Faye can call you?"

"I guess. But I don't have a kid seat or anything."

"I'll leave mine." AJ had to fight to not choke up. What the hell?

"Are you going to cry like a—"

"I rode Killer Storm." No need to say more. He'd broken bones and not complained. Nothing was going to leak out of his eyes now. Thank God and little green apples, Marlena showed up with big bowls of Cowboy Casserole. He and Danny ate and talked about men they'd known in the rodeo. They also talked about which bulls AJ should consider riding to put him in the money. They both turned down the pie that seemed popular, although AJ nearly took a piece for later. He thought better of it when he realized he'd have to hide it. Boxes of candy were easy. Pie, not so much.

"I still have to wonder why you're here. I mean, you're selling the ranch, right?"

"Easier than other options."

"Could be. But you never really said what might be going on between you and Pepper. Claudette said—"

"We're housemates. My God, she and her mother are sharing a room. Me being on the road will be a good thing."

"As you well know, Faye lived in a commune. Her idea of what's right and proper isn't quite the same as most folks around here." Danny gave him a level stare, his blue eyes boring into AJ's brain.

"No one's business."

"You dog. I knew there was another reason you were hanging around."

"I told you why I'm here."

"Yep. You said it was easy." Danny actually waggled his eyebrows. AJ wanted to reach across the faded Formica tabletop and strangle him. What went on between him and Pepper was private.

"Nothing is going on," he said evenly, hoping to shut Danny up.

"That's not the AJ I know."

"That AJ is long gone. Disappeared as soon as I found out I had a daughter."

"Not so sure. After all, there's you and—"

This time he didn't stop himself. His hand shot across the table and snatched at Danny's collar, twisting it. "I told you it's none of your business, if there was anything going on. And there isn't. Do you understand?"

"Boys," Marlena said. "What's that sign say? Take it outside."

AJ let go, stood and stared hard at Danny. "I expect you to answer your phone. And I expect you to treat Pepper with respect."

Danny somehow looked unruffled but a knowing smile stretched his lips just before he said, "Hot damn. Lavonda is going to owe me fifty dollars."

Chapter Twelve

"Did you ask the mayor to call me?" Pepper inquired as she and AJ made a final tour of the crops. Ella-Jayne was settled for the night with Butch curled up on the floor near her playpen that doubled as a makeshift crib. Faye was in the living room watching a movie. The ranch felt strangely quiet. Expectant. AJ left tomorrow. Her feelings about that were complex.

"I talked with him about being on call if you needed anything."

"This was about the garden and a grant that would allow me to rehab lots in town. I've been asking him about the town gardens for weeks."

"Nope. Didn't say anything about any of that."

Could something finally be going her way? Something other than AJ leaving. And she only cared about that because it meant she had another responsibility to add to the teetering stack. The little sting right around her heart had nothing to do with anything. They stopped at the end of the row. Now what?

"Dave said I could swing by in two weeks." She nodded. "I'll try to call every night but on show nights, it might not happen. I don't know what I'll be up against. He's only had temp wranglers, and I got the feeling things are a mess. On a couple of venues, he'll be the producer, too." She nodded again. "I wouldn't be doing this unless I had to."

"You love the rodeo. I understand." Her brain understood. Other parts of her didn't get why he needed to leave, especially why he had to risk everything to crawl onto the back of an angry bull.

"I loved the rodeo. It got me out of Pinetown. I was good at it. Not the best but darned good. Danny was better. I made it into the money, though. I was really good with the stock and…it doesn't matter. Once I found out about EllaJayne, I couldn't be on the road. I had to look after her."

"Yet, here you are going out again."

"Only because I know you and Grammy Marie and Faye will keep her safe. I would never go if I didn't have you all."

She shouldn't feel so proud of herself. He'd say anything to get her to care for his daughter so he could go play the cowboy. Except she knew that wasn't true. He wasn't a liar. Just like Daddy Gene. He'd always been honest, even when she hadn't wanted to hear it.

"I'll check on the herd one more time, then I'd better hit the hay. I've got a long day tomorrow." He didn't move.

She didn't want him to leave. She didn't want to be the one stuck at home worrying about him. She didn't want to care. "They'll miss you. Butch, too, and EllaJayne."

"I'll miss them, too," he said gruffly.

Pepper took in the final rays of the spectacular sunset. The Arizona skies regularly put on a show of magentas, oranges and purples. Tonight's seemed particularly vivid. The colors highlighted AJ's strong nose and cheekbones and the softness of his lips. His eyes were no longer on the faraway herd or the crop. They were on her, his stormy gray gaze searching her face for…what?

"I might even miss you," he said quietly, touching her face slowly and gently. She could have moved, stepped away. She didn't. She wanted the rough softness of his touch on her. She hadn't allowed herself that until this moment. She moved into his embrace. Opening to him and to his kiss.

Lordy be, this cowboy could kiss, warming her from the tips of her toes to the ends of her hair. She melted into the heat of his tongue. His hands roamed her back and down to her butt, yanking her hard against him, just where she wanted to be.

"I might miss you, too," she whispered against his ear when she could finally pull away enough to catch her breath. "I won't miss you hogging the bathroom in the morning, though." She squeezed him hard, not wanting to let go even as she tried to give herself space to breathe. To keep her heart and her head together. "I won't miss hiding your stash of Spam from Faye. No one actually wants to eat that." She felt giddy from the lack of oxygen and the heat of his hands on her back and hips. How could he surround her with warmth that was so different from the lingering heat of the summer day?

"Spam is cowboy ambrosia. I noticed at least one of my cans was missing," he whispered against her temple. "I should've reported you to Chief Rudy. Maybe I'll just take it out in trade." His mouth nuzzled down her neck and his hand traced up her waist until it landed on her breast. "Tit for tat."

She laughed out loud—freely, happily. "What are you—" She couldn't say more because his hands and lips stole her breath and her reason…again. "Oh," she whispered when she realized that her shirt was open and his hand was inside her bra. When had that happened?

"Pepper, I have to… Come with me." He clasped her hand and dragged her toward his truck. He'd bought a second-hand capper to transform the bed of the pickup into a Hillbilly RV. She hesitated for a moment, not sure she wanted another memory of them together, skin to skin and heart to heart.

"AJ. Wait."

"What's wrong?" He turned his storm-cloud gaze on hers, edgy with desire and want. Was that enough? Was that what she wanted?

"You're leaving."

"I'm just traveling."

"I know. You'll be back when you can." What did that mean for her? For the ache that filled her chest?

"Pepper, honey," he said, pulling her to him, chest to chest. Not one millimeter of air seeped between them. He kissed her again and just like that every-thing fell into place. She needed and wanted him to-night. Tomorrow would take care of itself.

"I've never been in a Hillbilly RV," she whispered against his mouth. "But I hope you put oil on those shocks."

"Really?" he said as he kissed the side of her face with gentle fun. "You expectin' to give them a work-out, honey?"

"Maybe. I plan to see if a bull rider is as good at being ridden."

He yanked her against him so she knew that he was ready, more than ready to meet every one of her demands. No, not demands. What she needed and what she wanted to give to him. And only him.

AJ HAD NEVER LAUGHED, teased and enjoyed the lead-up to getting horizontal so much. Pepper made it so easy—and so hard. He laughed at himself, then she used her hand to remind him what they would be doing in…he didn't care how soon or how long from now because every moment took forever and that was just fine with him.

"Into the RV you go," he said, helping her into the bed of the pickup that had been transformed into something like living quarters. Well, a place to sleep on the road. He laid her back on the nest of blankets and pillows, looking like a woman ready for him to love. Damn.

"What are you waiting for?" she said with a saucy smile as she arched her back and took off her bra.

In the dimness lit only by the glow of the barn light, he caught glimpses of Pepper. He lowered his head to her breast, nuzzling there as his hand moved to the waistband of her jeans. "Oh, darlin', I was just waitin' for you," he said, his drawl thickening his words as his finger delved between her thighs and found her more than ready. Dear Lord. She writhed as his fingers discovered that place he knew could set her off. He'd found it on the lounge and had dreamed about making her—

"Not yet," she gasped holding his hand still. "I told you I'm going to test your mettle."

"My mettle?" His brain fogged with the smell and feel of her.

She sat up and pushed him back. He didn't protest. He kept his grip tight on her, though. He didn't want her to be more than inches from him. Her clever hands and mouth made time speed up and slow down all at once. Finally, she stopped, found his condoms, then said, "You know cowgirls go for more than eight seconds."

"Really?"

"Really." She lifted herself up and over him. Settling down as he thrust up. "Giddy up," she gasped as she moved her hips.

Afterward, he held Pepper close, her limp body sprawled over his. He didn't want to break whatever spell had landed on them. For the first time in his life, his heart fluttered not with the thought of doing what they'd just done again…though they'd be doing that. Hell, yes. He'd pictured clearly, him on the phone talking to her—not dirty talk. Just everyday talk like they'd had in the evenings in the garden. It wasn't sexy, but it still made his heart thud. What the hell was that about? Then he heard Gene. The Gene he'd known as a teenager when he'd first hit the rodeo circuit. "You know how you know you're hitched to the right woman?" he'd counseled AJ after an ugly split with a barrel racer. "You want to talk with her. Not the kind of talk that'll get you between the sheets. It'll be the woman who makes the everyday extraordinary. That's when you'll know."

Sheep tails. Pepper made the everyday extraordinary. Why else did he want to go out into the garden with her every night? Why else did he share his Spam? Did he love her?

PEPPER GLUED HER gaze to the folder balanced on her knees while she listened to her patient. So far only one person this morning was not a member of the AJ fan club. Most of the town watched him whenever he rode and had adopted him as one of their own. Her current patient went over twist by turn every second of AJ's soon-to-be famous ride. What she and none of the others talked about was how he'd limped out of the arena. What had he done to himself? Not that it was Pepper's business. The rodeo had doctors. Three more days until he came back to Santa Faye Ranch.

"Shame it wasn't a big money ride."

Shame, indeed. "Wilma, I don't like these reports."

The middle-aged woman had a more than comfortable roll of spare weight around her waist and swollen ankles. It wasn't just her name that had an old-fashioned flair. She had the blood test numbers of the octogenarian her name reminded Pepper of—

"Just give me a pill."

"Instead of a pill, you need to eat better."

"Uh-huh." She agreed. "When did you say AJ's coming back?"

"I didn't. I know things are tight. I have a crop coming in and I'd love to give you some—"

"Harold doesn't like it."

"You don't even know what I'm going to say."

"He won't like it. You know how it is. If it doesn't come in a can or box or had a hoof before it was packed in Styrofoam, he ain't got no interest."

"I understand, but maybe just one part of the meal?"

"We don't need the help," the woman said stubbornly, even though Pepper knew that she shopped at the food bank in the next town and the dented-can aisle at the big grocery outlet. Gossip didn't just run to AJ and his bull riding.

"Maybe you could come out and help next week? We'll be picking beans, and Faye—" here Pepper paused for strength "—is shearing her herd and wants some help spinning."

"Spinning? This is the 21st century. If I want yarn, I go to the Mountain of Crafts. I like making baby blankets for the children over in Siberia." There was a group of women who got together to knit and crochet and sometimes even quilt.

"Would your Angel Bee like the yarn?"

"Maybe," Wilma said slowly. "I'll ask. It's just that the other yarn is so bright and pretty."

"I understand."

"I'll ask and I'll be out to help pick beans. It's been dogs' years since I did that. We had a garden in Iowa when I was a kid. I hated weeding so I never wanted to have one after I got married. Harold feels the same way."

"It is a little bit of work. But the mayor and I are looking at a garden in town, with raised beds that wouldn't have weeds. It would be close to home and you could grow whatever you wanted."

Wilma didn't say no. Pepper figured that was a victory. She gave the woman some free samples of a new blood pressure medicine she hoped would help. If Wilma and Harold didn't change their diet, the pills wouldn't make much of a long-term difference. Pepper made a mental note to work on the woman when she came out to help at the ranch.

TODAY THE CLOSED clinic was as quiet as it could be with a toddler and dog racing around the waiting room. Pepper had stopped in for just a minute to pick up a file. "EllaJayne. Butch. Stop running, please." She looked through her desk, the file wasn't where it should be. She couldn't leave the dog and girl alone very long. The destruction they could wreak in seconds was awesome in its breadth and depth. When she finally found what she was looking for, tucked inside another unrelated folder, Pepper's gut told her something was wrong. The clinic was quiet. Too quiet for a dog and a girl to not be getting in any trouble.

"EllaJayne," she said as she walked toward the waiting area. It was empty...except for the toppled basket of magazines and a small ficus tree on its side spilling dirt everywhere. The front door was open. Crap. How could she have forgotten the girl's magician abilities?

"EllaJayne. Butch," Pepper yelled, trying not to sound mad. She didn't want them to hide or run from her because they feared punishment. At this point, she wasn't sure what she'd do when she found them. She looked up and down the street and still didn't see them. "Think, Pepper. Think." The diner? Pepper had braved the place for a treat for the little girl the few times they'd come into town during the six weeks her daddy had been gone. Pepper raced down the sidewalk sweeping her gaze around the town, hoping to catch a glimpse of the girl. What had she been wearing? That was the first thing the police always asked.

"Whoa," Danny said as he caught her arm, half a block from the town hall. "Didn't you hear me call your name?"

"EllaJayne," she gasped. "I can't find her."

"She's at the office," Danny said with a gentle voice. "Her and that useless dog. He tried to bite me."

She didn't wait for him to say more but raced to the town hall, wrenching open the door and moving toward the sound of the girl's sobs. "EllaJayne." Had she'd been hurt? The sobs' volume turned to eleven and Butch yipped anxiously before he growled with menace.

"Pepper Moonbeam, get in here and calm down your danged dog," Chief Rudy's deep voice boomed out.

She ran through mud and molasses as she tried to reach Baby Girl. "EllaJayne."

"Peep," a watery sob came back.

Almost there. She moved as fast as her uncooperative legs allowed her through the police department's door. There was EllaJayne behind the reception desk with Butch guarding her.

"Peep," EllaJayne squealed and ran toward her, the sobs rising in volume again, along with Butch's now ecstatic yips.

Pepper dropped to her knees and opened her arms. The little girl threw herself against her, her body quivering with her cries. Butch licked her ear. "It's okay. I've got you, baby," Pepper whispered to EllaJayne, cupping her head into the hollow of her shoulder rocking the two of them. "Shh, sweetie. It's all right.

You're safe." Pepper buried her own face into the top of the girl's head to calm her own racing heart.

"The mayor found them ready to cross the street," Chief Rudy said sternly.

Pepper's heart clenched. Oh, God. She could see the disasters. A car hitting them, hurling them into the air. She clutched EllaJayne closer to her. "She opened the door at the clinic. I was just in the—" Her words dribbled to a stop. She sounded just like AJ when she'd first met him. The little girl really was a quick-escape artist. She understood better his fear, frustration and defeat. Pepper slowly released EllaJayne to stand.

"Déjà vu all over again, huh?" Danny said.

Pepper nodded her head, looking down at the two escapees. Now, her fear was transforming into something not quite so pretty. She wanted to shake both of them. EllaJayne's tear-streaked face hurt Pepper's heart. Butch turned his head to the side, looking ashamed. Those faces. How could she do anything but hold them tight? She sighed deeply.

Chief Rudy said, "Maybe a bell on them?"

A laugh burbled up from her churning insides. "Or one of those things that's supposed to help you find your keys?"

Danny smiled. "I think Lem's store has them. That better be your next stop."

EllaJayne giggled along with the adults, and Butch waggled his butt in excitement. "Thanks, Danny. I don't know what… Thanks." She looked again at EllaJayne. The toddler who'd wriggled her way into Pepper's heart. Darn it. This was not the way her life was supposed to go. Pepper shook her head. Time to go home and focus on what would matter when the girl and her father left Pepper. The garden, the community. Those would fill up that hole.

"Peep. Wuv you."

Pepper gulped back a sob of her own.

Chapter Thirteen

AJ leaned back on the pillows in his Hillbilly RV, enjoying the scent of bee balm Faye insisted would strengthen his Taurus tendencies. He didn't think the scent or the special tea she'd sent with him had changed the outcome of any of his rides. Still, he didn't throw it away. Just knowing someone thought about him and cared enough to help did something for him. He shook his head to get rid of those stupid notions. He'd soon be selling and moving on. Then his "real" life would begin with EllaJayne and a job that didn't batter his already hurting body.

He checked the time. Two minutes until he could videochat on his phone with his daughter. He could see in the month and more he'd been away that she'd changed. She could point at objects in the room and tell him what they were. He'd also swear she'd gotten inches taller. He rubbed at his sore shoulder—yanked by a reluctant bull—and wondered if the bruise on his cheek had turned a darker color. Pepper would notice. She always noticed. Time to call and not think about what Pepper's attention meant to him.

"Daddy," EllaJayne said when their videochat started. While he still didn't think he was her absolute favorite person, she seemed genuinely excited to see and speak with him. The picture disappeared as she said, "Boo-boo." He guessed she was patting the bruise she saw on his face.

Well, that answered his question about the bruise. "It's okay, baby," he said, seeing her frown.

"Peep. Boo-boo."

"Daddy's boo-boo is fine. Did you pet Boot today?" he asked. His daughter nodded her head, pointing and telling him what she saw, the growing skill with language something he'd missed being a part of, except through a phone screen.

"We need to tell Daddy about you running away today? Right?" Pepper finally said.

"What?" AJ's heart lurched.

Pepper picked up EllaJayne and sat down with her so the two of them could talk with him. "She and Boot went exploring. But I told her the rules. No going off on her own." His daughter shook her head no, the dark fall of hair swinging. "Next time you'll wait for Pepper or Grana or Daddy. Right?" EllaJayne nodded vigorously along with Pepper.

AJ wanted to find out more about what had happened but he knew getting the full story from the little girl wouldn't happen. He listened for another few minutes, then too soon, Pepper said, "Kiss Daddy good-night. Butch is ready to go lie down." That was the new routine he was missing for getting his daughter to *b-e-d*.

"Night, Daddy," she said as she leaned forward so only the top of her head showed. He heard the loud juicy kiss. He smiled feeling the virtual touch deep in his heart.

"Night, Baby Girl." EllaJayne ran off yelling for Boot. Pepper's face appeared on the screen both concerned and a little fearful.

"You probably guessed that we had an adventure today?"

He nodded, waiting for her to explain.

"I took EllaJayne and Butch with me to the clinic. I needed to pick up a folder. I was in my office—for thirty seconds tops—and she opened the front door and got out." Pepper said all that in a rush full of fear and self-reproach.

"Of anyone, I know what a magician that kid is with doors," he said, almost feeling pride in his daughter's scary talent.

"She and Butch were ready to cross the street when they were caught. She wanted to see the animals from the picture over the Emporium. That took me a while to figure out." Pepper sealed her lips, obviously trying to not cry. "I was so scared. I could imagine everything that could have happened."

"Oh, Pepper, baby," he whispered. He ached to pull her into his arms. "You did everything you could to keep her safe."

"Don't be so nice. You should be yelling at me," she accused wetly.

He touched his fingers to the screen, trying to reach through the danged phone. "Don't cry, please. I can't stand seeing you cry," he whispered.

"I'm sorry. It's just—" she swallowed another sob.

"I know, honey," he said softly. God, he couldn't stand this being away from the ranch and from his girls. He was in deep. "Hush, now. It's all right."

"I know I'm being stupid," she said fiercely, wiping at her face. "And don't think I didn't notice that bruise. Did you put ice on it?"

Now, she sounded more like the Pepper he knew. "Not yet." He wouldn't tell her that his plan was to hold a cold beer against it. He had one left in his cooler.

"How's the back and hip?"

"Well enough. How are the Beauties?" He wanted to distract her from her interrogation.

"Still not apologizing for spitting at Danny."

He laughed a little. "They don't seem like the kind of critters who feel regret."

"They will when we shear them and all of the other animals laugh at them being naked."

Great. She'd said naked and he wasn't picturing alpacas or llamas. He was long past being a teenager so why did she make him feel that way? "No one would laugh at you."

"We weren't talking about me," she said sternly, then her face softened and her eyes heated. "Plus, I don't think you've entirely seen me like that."

"Could be. Should we solve that problem now?"

She pulled in a breath. "I don't... How can you make me go from crying to—"

"To hot—"

"No," she said on an embarrassed laugh. "Time to say good-night. Put ice on that cheek and maybe use some on your little bronc, too."

"My little bronc? That's just cruel, woman." They both laughed. It felt good to enjoy a little sexy teasing, almost like they were a couple. Except they weren't. He sobered instantly. "Well, then, good night."

"Good night," she agreed. "We'll talk tomorrow." She switched off the chat.

Two more weeks until he was back at Santa Faye Ranch. By then, he needed to get himself in control and remember that their...whatever it was had a sell-by date. She understood that, and he was happy that she wasn't holding him to anything more than short-term fun, right? He needed his beer and not just to ice his face.

PEPPER COULDN'T BELIEVE all the "helpers" who'd come out today. The small field was filled with people picking beans and weeding and even planting the next crop. More amazing was the crew helping with shearing the Beauties. The cluster of ladies outside the corral eyed the beasts with greed. Apparently, Wilma's Angel Bee had connections to a co-op of spinners and weavers who would, for a percentage of the fleece, take care of spinning the fiber. Then they'd show the Angel Bee ladies how to dye it so they could use if for their own projects.

Faye, for maybe the first time since they had moved to the town two decades ago, was fitting in comfortably. People didn't even roll their eyes at her tofu snacks. Of course, that might be because they were outnumbered by a covered dish spread rivaling the one from a Fourth of July fifty years ago that was so legendary oldsters still drooled when they talked about it.

What Pepper was thinking about, though, was AJ's return. His late return. He'd stayed longer on the road than he'd initially promised. Today, she'd been asked a dozen times when he was expected. A second successful ride had moved him to hero-of-Angel-Crossing status. He'd called almost every evening as promised and spoken with EllaJayne. Of course, a toddler couldn't answer the phone or say much. Usually, Pepper filled in the conversational gaps. Sometimes he called very late, after EllaJayne was asleep, so they talked. Sometimes they even had what Pepper had been calling in her head "adult" talks. Ones that left her hot and bothered. Worse, they usually led to steamy dreams featuring AJ without a shirt and saying silly things like he loved her. She even said that she loved him back. Good thing she didn't believe her dreams meant anything more than she'd been speaking with him before she fell asleep.

What a disaster. She barely had time for her career and the farm. How would she squeeze in a boyfriend? Could a man with a child even be a boyfriend? How did that work? Besides, she had to remember that he was going to sell the ranch.

Butch dashed by, followed by an overly excited EllaJayne. Pepper chuckled and went back to sorting the beans and other produce that had been donated by a nearby grocery store. She wasn't calling any of it a donation, though. These were samples and giveaways.

Butch barked furiously, running to the barn and back, with EllaJayne trying to catch up. Pepper could see the disaster coming. The little girl would soon be crying or screaming.

"Butch," she called as she walked toward the duo. The dog listened as well as he usually did, which was not at all. "EllaJayne, sweetie, come here."

The girl turned, frowned, pointed and said, "Boot. Daddy."

While Pepper's grasp of the toddler's vocabulary had gotten better, she didn't get all the nuances. Had AJ been gone so long EllaJayne thought the dog was her father? Butch galloped up, sat, barked and raced away. The girl tried to follow, but Pepper took hold of her because the dog had started down the drive.

Butch raced back and sat panting at her feet. EllaJayne hugged him, repeating, "Daddy. Daddy." What was wrong with them? Then she heard it. A pickup truck. It could be one of a hundred trucks from around the area. Not everyone from town had come out to the ranch, even if it looked that way.

She refused to think or let her heart leap at the idea it might be AJ. She was better than a toddler and certainly smarter than a cattle dog who thought he was a poodle. Except it was AJ and her heart did a fluttery leap and she couldn't make it stop.

AJ CURSED LONG and foul. He'd need to break that habit…again. This was not the homecoming he'd imagined. He'd pictured saying hello to Pepper and EllaJayne. Then Baby Girl and Faye would be picked up by Danny so they could go on a road trip for a few hours, while he and Pepper finished what they'd started during their phone calls. Instead the ranch was filled with people. It looked like the entire town was there. He parked his pickup in a line of six others.

He got his bag from the king cab and sucked in a long breath to stop the roil of nerves from his chest to his gut. He settled his hat and adjusted his sunglasses. None of it mattered when Butch hit him, quickly followed by EllaJayne, who launched herself at him, wrapping her arms and legs boa-constrictor style around his torso when he bent to her. She squeezed him hard and repeated with a shrill excitement: "Daddy."

"She and Butch heard you before anyone else," Pepper said when she strolled up. "Let Daddy breathe, honey," she coaxed, then went on, "Your drive was okay?"

He didn't want to be disappointed she hadn't greeted him as enthusiastically as his daughter. They weren't an item, and the entire town, including her patients, clustered nearby. "Trip was good," he said. "What's all of this?" He motioned with his head toward the garden and the corral. Why hadn't she said anything?

"The first harvest in the garden and the Great Fleecing—that's what Faye is calling it. We found a use for all of that fuzz. I didn't tell you because I didn't want you to feel like you had to come home for any of it."

"I wish you would have told me," he said, his gaze locking back onto her. He'd forgotten the warm richness of her hair and the invitation in every curve of her body.

She shrugged. "Everyone insisted on bringing food. You hungry?"

"Nah. Better put away my gear, then I'll help." EllaJayne pulled hard on the thumb in her mouth, her head heavy on his shoulder. He couldn't stop gazing at Pepper.

"AJ," Danny shouted from ten feet away, breaking his concentration. "Saw your last ride. Nice. Made it into the money."

He had and now it didn't matter because he'd—

"I'm Harold and I just want to say that we're proud to have you here in Angel Crossing. I mean the mayor was famous and all but that was years ago. Now, we've got ourselves a real live bull rider."

AJ's SHOULDER SMARTED from the back slaps that went with the congratulations he'd gotten as he'd helped with the Beauties. He followed up that excitement with spreading manure and preparing another field. This one for "fall" crops—peas and broccoli. Not his favorites. Now, if they were prepping for a Fiddle Faddle field or a Spam tree, he'd think it was time well spent. But he knew what Pepper was doing would make a difference for Angel Crossing. The fresh produce was important. He was *not* that big an idiot. He could also see having everyone out here helping was just as important. The little town, like his own in Kentucky, was struggling not only with providing jobs but also with losing its heart. Angel Crossing still had a chance. Not that he'd be here to see that or see Pepper's vision become reality. He hadn't said it, but he hoped she knew she and Faye could live here and farm the land until the place sold.

"Arthur John," Faye called from a long stretch of food. "Marla made Spam salad just for you."

He wished Faye would stop calling him by his full name. He wasn't that man. Never had been. He was AJ, hell-raiser and bull rider. He saw EllaJayne in Pepper's arms. The two looked natural together and Baby Girl could have been hers, theirs. Damn. No more swearing. He blanked out his thoughts and focused on right here and now by enjoying the food, the beer and even the congratulations, but none of it would last.

"FAYE FOUND HER TRIBE," Pepper said as they watched her mother wave to the crew of women who had helped turn some of the Beauties' fleece into yarn. They'd made plans for a dye-in and spin-a-thon in a couple of weeks.

"Could be," he said. His back had started to ache an hour ago and his ribs burned from where they'd been bruised by a shove from a bull who hadn't wanted to cooperate. He'd had fantasies of taking Pepper to bed—a big soft bed—not a tiny lounge or in the back of his pickup.

"What?" Pepper asked.

"Nothing. Just a long day. Not just for me, either. Time for—" he stopped before he said the most dreaded word in EllaJayne's world, which directly led to long tantrums and negotiating.

"I'll take care of that. You haven't even had a chance to unpack."

Pepper left him alone, looking out over the land that was his now. He'd gotten word from Bobby Ames that the estate was settled. He could put it on the market and then move on. California. Maybe Oregon. Both places could use cowboys, and he already had friends there. *Just like in Angel Crossing.* Gene's voice filled his mind. Dang, that was creepy.

"So good to have you back, Arthur John."

"It's AJ," he told Faye again. Butch had followed her over and sat on his foot. The dog had been trying to stick as close as he could, between the temptation of dropped food from the buffet and the pull of a passel of kids willing to rub his belly and throw a toy.

"We missed you. Your male energy is important to the ranch."

"I'm happy to be here." For how long was the question. AJ hadn't even told his boss Dave about his change in fortune. Why not? He should be shouting all this from the top of the pickup that the ranch was *his*. Finally, luck or his sign or whatever was going his way.

"You know Gene had a plan."

"Yes, ma'am."

"When he got sick again—" she choked off the words, her eyes glistening with tears. Butch moved from AJ's foot to lean against Faye. "He knew. We knew his time wasn't long. We talked. We laughed. We even made love." Tears rolled down her cheeks and AJ wasn't sure what to do. He'd never known what to do when women cried, but he stepped forward and pulled her into a one-armed hug. Faye was stiff and went on, "I've got to get the rest of this out. Pepper's making this work. She's found her place here. She's finally accepted that people wanted her, not just her skills, and didn't judge her…well, not too much…for how we lived. I knew it would be difficult for her, but I knew it would make her both tough and compassionate."

My God, Faye sounded almost like a normal mother. "She's definitely both. Look what she did today." His gaze took in the harvested and prepped fields. He smiled at the shorn llamas and alpacas, looking slightly embarrassed by their new haircuts.

"Did she tell you that our little one is starting to use her crayons and markers? I think she may be an artist. She's an old soul. You know that, right?"

The Faye he knew was back. "So you've said."

"She'll be sleeping with me tonight."

"Pardon?" he said because what else could he say?

"I think EllaJayne needs some Grana time." She cocked her head to the side, looking a lot like Pepper when she was trying to find an argument to get her own way. "And because I've been told it's icky, I'm not saying anything else, especially not about you and Pepper."

"Jeez."

"Everyone knows you're a couple. We all expected to find you'd gone missing at some point during the party."

"What do you mean everyone knows?" The entire town knew he and Pepper had done...crap. This was a horror fest.

"You can't hide that kind of thing. Everyone approves by the way." She patted Butch's head as she pulled away from AJ, her expression calm and the tears dried. "Gene approves, too, in his own way. Pepper is his daughter, after all." Faye walked away, her long skirts swirling. Butch stared at AJ, yipped, then ran after Faye.

He cursed long and foul again. He'd mend his ways tomorrow. What the hell did he do now?

Chapter Fourteen

Pepper stood in the living room staring at the crooked bookcase, her brain working really hard to get her body and her heart in line. Faye had taken EllaJayne to the bedroom for a slumber party and "a little Grana time." Why couldn't Faye be a disapproving, you-won't-have-sex-until-you're-married kind of mom? Because then she wouldn't be Faye.

"So, Faye and EllaJayne are having a party?" AJ's voice came from the other side of the couch, close enough that she could smell his unique cowboy mix of dust and leather.

"They just went into *b-e-d*."

"You don't have to spell it out for me." His mouth curved in a half smile, but his eyes were a grim gray. He took a step and stiffened abruptly.

"Your back? Hip?" she asked. His apparent pain putting her back on familiar and comfortable territory. Physician's Assistant Pepper to the rescue. She'd take care of this and that would put the distance back between them.

"It's nothing. I just need to get to bed. Long day. Long week." He didn't move and his posture stayed stiff.

"How about a little ice? Then I'll get the heating pad. Daddy Gene used it for his back, too."

AJ frowned. "I'd rather go with aspirin and beer."

"You know what I think of that home remedy. Lie down on the couch and I'll get the—"

"I'm not your patient. If I need to doctor my back, I'll do it myself."

"I know where your daughter gets her 'me do it' gene." She stared at him with her most intimidating PA glare. He glared right back. "Fine. I've got things to take care of, then I'm going to bed." She swallowed and plowed on. "If you can't wake Faye, let me know, and I'll get EllaJayne for you."

"She said everyone thinks we're a couple."

Pepper gave a half shrug. "Faye also decides when to grocery-shop based on her horoscope."

"She didn't seem surprised or upset."

Pepper closed her eyes so she wouldn't see the ridicule in AJ's eyes. Then his scent and his heat were beside her. How had he moved so quickly?

Without touching her, he whispered in her ear, "I might not understand astrology, but I do understand I want you. I've wanted you every night."

Her breath caught in her throat on the hunger in his voice, on the yearning racing through her body. "I want…I need…what we had when we talked."

"Nothing shameful in that," he said across the suddenly sensitive skin of her cheek.

"Nothing," she agreed. "An adult woman chooses her own partner when and where she wants."

"Absolutely." He pulled her close for a deep kiss, wringing a moan from her. "Only this time we're not doing it on patio furniture or in the back of my truck. We're using a bed…and I refuse to feel weird about it."

She laughed. Nervous and turned-on. "A bed. I can do that. I want to do that." He pulled her to him without another word and kissed her again until she couldn't breathe. Then she pushed back enough to say, "I just want you to know that I understand it doesn't mean—"

"We're not talking anymore. We've talked enough."

She couldn't argue with that.

PEPPER HAD LEARNED in high school you couldn't die from embarrassment—even if it felt that way. She reminded herself of that as she made her way to the kitchen for coffee. She'd woken on her own and hoped it was late enough that everyone had gone to do something that meant she wouldn't have to face them until later. She heard the whole household including Butch. She could do this. Whatever she and AJ had done last night wasn't wrong. They were adults. They were free and single. They were responsible. She really needed coffee.

"Peep, mine," EllaJayne said as she held out a handful of Oaty-O's from her high chair. The little girl only got the meaning of "mine" about half of the time.

"Thanks," Pepper said, taking an O and munching it with grinning pleasure. EllaJayne squeaked out her delight and Butch pressed against Pepper's leg. She refused to look at the two other people in the room. She made herself walk without rushing to the coffeepot.

"Sweetie, fire and earth signs bond strongly and

securely," Faye said out of the blue. Pepper glanced over to AJ now feeding his daughter and ignoring everything but the spoon of yogurt. "You know, those signs make good couples or partners, whether friends or lovers. Now, Pepper, you should have juice and yogurt to rebalance your chemistry. I've already told Arthur John he needs to eat double protein to replenish—"

"Faye," both she and AJ said with an equal amount of dismay.

EllaJayne frowned and looked fiercely at Faye. "Bad Grana," she added.

"What?" Faye asked with her own brand of innocence and hurt.

"We don't… It's none of your business," Pepper finally settled on. She glanced at AJ and caught him watching her, a look on his face that made her heart flutter in a way that made her think of forever.

"I was going to say to replenish the muscles he injured on the road." Faye stood regally. "EllaJayne, Butch and I will go outside since you two refuse to talk with us here. You need to iron out the evening and then Pepper, sweetie, you need to tell Arthur John about the mayor's plan." Faye gathered up the baby and the dog and went swishing out of the house.

AJ got up slowly to put his daughter's dishes in the sink and refill his coffee.

"I can write you a prescription for muscle relaxants."

"I told you before aspirin is enough. It's just that I… We… God, this is awkward."

"Welcome back to my world. You've already met

Faye." She kept her gaze on the milky brown swirl of coffee.

"So what are we doing here?" he asked his voice belligerent.

"I assume you mean besides having morning-after coffee?"

"This isn't our first morning after, so why is it so awkward?"

"Faye. She has that talent."

He shook his head. "It's us. I think we both knew what would happen when I got back here. We wouldn't have talked on the phone like that otherwise."

There was that. "Faye knows. Butch knows. Even EllaJayne knows something's up."

"According to your mama, everyone knew what was going on before I even rolled into the ranch."

"Maybe." She thought there was something else. Something he wanted her to pull out of him.

He opened the fridge and kept his head inside as he said, "I'm home for three days, then back on the road for three weeks." She waited for him to say whatever he was building up to. What if he wasn't looking for a repeat of what they'd done in the bed? What if he'd found someone else? Why would he have—

"I got a call from Bobby Ames."

The ranch. This was about the ranch. "You did?" she said, trying for nonchalance. "He didn't say anything when I saw him in town."

"He's a lawyer. There are rules." She waited again. He stood with a loaf of bread in one hand. "The estate has settled, and I'm putting the ranch on the market. The whole ranch."

He'd known that last night. While he'd made love

to her, he'd known he would be breaking her heart today. No matter she knew this day would come. She'd hoped he'd change his mind about at least giving her a chance to buy the house and the acreage around it. Not because they'd slept together but because it was only fair.

"That's okay. Danny helped me find a grant to create the gardens we need in town. He and I have been working on a plan."

"You and Danny, huh?"

"He understands how important this is to me and to Angel Crossing."

"Good to know." AJ said as he crushed the loaf of bread. "I need to check my equipment."

So much for Faye's prediction about their signs and compatibility.

AJ HAD HIT the road a day early and ended up with nothing more than an aching back and a hangover. Pepper and Santa Faye Ranch weren't his future and it was good he'd figured that out. He still owed his ex her money. The rides hadn't netted him as much as he'd expected. He'd thought he might get away with splitting up the ranch, but he needed to sell it quickly. He'd been told that would be easier if he kept the acreage intact. Once he sold the ranch he'd give Suzy the final payout, go to court and get full custody with no strings attached. Then he'd be done with her and Kentucky. His step after that was still hazy. He had a lead on at least one job, but maybe he should buy land of his own. But if he was going to buy land, why not just stay in Angel Crossing? He could sell off a portion of the ranch, just like Pepper had asked, even if it took a little longer to sell the rest of it. Except he wouldn't have enough to pay off Suzy.

If he stayed to raise cattle and horses—once he learned how—and…marry Pepper. Yeah, right, like that was happening. So they'd done the midnight do-si-do? Didn't mean anything. He'd done that particular dance with plenty of other women, except the other women hadn't made him want to settle his butt down. To come home to the same person, to wake to the same face on the pillow. When they'd woken in bed together—the first for them—for a second he'd seen the mornings stretched out before them and he hadn't wanted to run away. It had looked like the best future he could imagine. Why not? Maybe because he'd be taking Pepper's ranch and her dreams from her. Since selling just a portion of the ranch wouldn't be enough to pay off Suzy and get him started on a new life, with a little nest egg for EllaJayne's future, he couldn't go down the path with Pepper toward something permanent. Even if that had begun to look mighty nice.

He checked his phone. Two more hours until he said he'd call home. Sheep tails. He couldn't think of Santa Faye Ranch as home. It wasn't. It was the cash cow, the top bull that would guarantee him his daughter and a fresh start. His lead on a ranch manager job was at a big place up in Oregon where they raised rodeo animals and ran a rodeo school. It seemed best to keep as far away from Kentucky as he could, not only because of Suzy. There were also the McCrearys. If they found out he had money, they'd be right there with their hands out.

DANG. HIS THUMB ached from the crushing it had taken. He hoped he wouldn't lose the nail. Faye would have a remedy. Probably having to do with the rising moon and mouse feet.

The producer of this event had gotten a cheap block of rooms, and AJ had "splurged," actually renting one of them. He couldn't face two more nights in the Hillbilly RV. His back and hip wouldn't take it. This near the end of the trip, he ached all over. Getting home…not home, but getting back to Arizona, meant being able to rest up a little as he put the ranch on the market and decided on his next job. His current contract was up at the end of the week. The work in Oregon was looking less shiny, too. No living quarters were included, and the place was more than fifty miles from the nearest town. Exactly how would he find someone to care for Baby Girl?

If it hadn't been thirty minutes until his nightly call to EllaJayne, he'd have headed to the honky-tonk across the parking lot for shots and a little uncomplicated company. Yep. It was the call keeping him from seeking out a good time.

He paced around the room and pushed his duffel back into the closet. His pocket vibrated. Crap, it would probably be a stock problem. The bull who'd been acting up earlier? He pulled out the phone and saw Pepper's name. That thud in his heart was not excitement.

"AJ?" she said.

"Who else?"

"I'm not telling him to find out the birth dates of the bulls, Faye." That comment had not been meant for him.

"Pepper, what's wrong?"

She went on, "We had a visitor today."

Faye's voice came through the phone, "Tell him our visitor has to be a Capricorn. He has all the signs of the goat and a rising—"

"I heard that. Who was there? Danny?"

"Why would you think Danny? He's been a big help."

Not much of a friend if he was swooping in to "solve" Pepper's problems. "Danny is a selfish—"

"It's not Danny. It's your family."

He stopped pacing. "My family? Gene had kids?"

"Your family from Kentucky. A cousin. Your father's step-brother's… I can't remember all of it. But he said that Suzy told him about the money you were paying her. Then he said if you didn't show your face and start ponying up, he was calling child services because your paperwork wasn't legal and you'd left your child with strangers."

Nevin. It had to be Nevin. He'd been after Suzy, too. The man had never worked a day in his life. He'd been using all his brain power since they were teens on schemes to get rich. Hell. This was bad. "He's there? At the ranch?"

"He's staying by the interstate. He came out today and—"

"He made EllaJayne cry and Butch tried to bite him. Good boy," Faye said loudly and the dog added a yip.

"Did he leave a number?"

"Yes, but why would he do this? I don't understand." Pepper sounded truly confused.

"Too complicated to explain. I'll call and straighten

him out." She wouldn't understand. Even with the challenges of Faye as a mother and Daddy Gene being her sort-of step-daddy, Pepper had had more love and support from them than he'd had in his whole blasted extended family. Pepper seemed to want to say more. Instead she put EllaJayne on the line.

He knew what he had to do as soon as this call was over. Call his cousin and figure out his price. His and Suzy's. They had to be in this together. He nearly had enough for this installment. The ranch couldn't sell fast enough so he'd be done with her and now Nevin.

He didn't have the right to drag Pepper into this mess. He'd take care of it on his own. He'd been doing that for a long time.

"Nevin," AJ said when his cousin picked up. "What the hell are you doing in Arizona?"

"Good, cuz, they did call you. Wasn't sure that hippie would remember."

"Just tell me what you want." AJ paced the tiny worn-out motel room.

"Seems Cousin Gene forgot he's got more family than you."

AJ didn't speak.

"You know us McCrearys. Share and share alike. Doesn't seem right he left everything to you."

"Get to the point, Nevin."

"Then there's your daughter. You took her from her mama without even telling her about the ranch. That's her daughter's inheritance. She wants to make sure her baby isn't cheated like Gene done to me and the rest of us."

The two of them had drawn a line through the

dots even faster than he would have thought possible. "Suzy signed the paper."

"She did but then she didn't know about the ranch or that you were leaving her precious baby with strangers."

They wanted money, obviously, but how much? All of it? He couldn't do that. "I didn't leave my daughter with strangers. The ladies were Gene's family, and we've been staying with them."

"You're not here now and haven't been here much for months. Doesn't seem much like the way a daddy should act, according to the courts and all."

AJ couldn't really argue with that, except the only reason he wasn't there was for his daughter. "Just tell me what the hell you want." He kept his voice low and even, clenching his fists and kicking the dresser.

"Obvious, ain't it? Suzy deserves at least half of the ranch, on top of what you already said you'd pay her, or she's going to the authorities and telling them how you kidnapped her baby. Her new lawyer said your agreement wouldn't hold up because she was under 'duress' when she signed it."

"Half the ranch. What else?"

"She don't like that agreement you made her sign. I know that ain't legal. Coercion. Read all about it on the internet. So she's not giving up her rights. She'll expect child support for being EllaJayne's mama, so that'll mean visits from the baby. You'll be moving back to Kentucky."

"She never wanted EllaJayne." His chest hurt from holding back the roar of words.

"Now, that ain't true. Post-whatever what not. Read about that, too, on the internet. We clear, cuz?"

"Clear as Kentucky moonshine."

"That woman said you have another week on the road. Guess that will be fine. I'll be here. Oh, now I remember the other thing. Since the ranch is yours, I think those women should be more hospitable-like. You know, open their home so I don't have to stay in this motel."

"Keep the hell away."

"That's not very friendly. Tell them I'll be by tomorrow."

AJ hung up and threw the phone across the room. He had to get to Arizona now. He picked up his duffel, shoved in his crap and left. If he drove all night, he'd be there by late morning. Maybe by then, he'd figure out what he could do to save his daughter and keep Nevin away from the ranch. He feared it meant ruining what he was only beginning to see he wanted his life to be.

Chapter Fifteen

Pepper dialed AJ again and got his voice mail. Her texts hadn't been answered, either. She wanted to talk with him about the yahoo who'd stopped by making threats. Luckily, she'd taken two days off and had been working in the garden when he'd shown up. Despite the visit, it'd been good to get outside and dig in the dirt. She'd be spending another day outside, too. The cooler temperatures of the approaching fall made the work pleasant, even though she'd spent a good part of the morning keeping EllaJayne out of trouble and fending off sloppy kisses from Butch.

The garden was doing well. Better, since Danny had all but promised the funding to move the project into town. He'd even suggested she add a flock of hens to eat bugs off the plants and to provide fresh eggs as part of her latest round of applications. The downside was that there was no way she could help turn the hens into fried chicken. She'd have to think on this longer. She pulled out her phone, hoping that AJ had called her back. Nothing.

"Daddy," EllaJayne yelled and Butch barked.

"Don't I wish," Pepper said softly, then told the little girl, "Pick the pretty flowers right here." Ella-

Jayne grinned widely. Pepper had sat her down in a patch of desert dandelion that had sprouted up between the rows. She figured that would keep the toddler busy for a little bit of time. Pepper went to work fast on the weeds among her plants. In less than a month, they'd have a crop of peas, garlic and peanuts. She needed to look on the internet for recipes. She should check with— Darn it. Someone was coming. Probably that Kentucky cousin. She gathered up EllaJayne and started herding Butch to the house. The little girl drummed her feet against Pepper's thighs yelling for her daddy. She could be as stubborn as one of the llamas.

"Daddy's at the rodeo, remember?" Pepper said in a reasonable voice. Like the toddler would respond to that.

Butch ran away. EllaJayne screamed for the dog.

"Lordy be, you two." She would take the toddler inside and then chase down the useless dog.

"I told you he'd come home," Faye said as she came out the front door and held out her arms for EllaJayne. "Go welcome him home."

Pepper turned. AJ stood by the truck, patting the dog, then strolled toward her. Oh, my, that was one fine man. Even if he was a cowboy like any other. The kind of man who didn't stick around.

Except she'd called and here he was. Yeah, well, he wouldn't have needed to be there if it hadn't been for his relatives. Of course he should have hightailed it home. The man was his problem.

"Nevin been back?" he asked when he was near.

She shook her head and looked him over. Exhausted and sore was her professional opinion. "Wait.

You were in Idaho? You couldn't have gotten here driving."

"Since that's where I was and I'm here now, guess I could have driven."

"You were on the road all night? That's dangerous. Why would you do that?" Pepper didn't know whether to be mad or wrap him in a hug. He did look rode hard and put away wet. And still he looked good. Not fair.

"I need coffee." He hesitated for a second by her, sighed deeply, then turned to Faye, who placed Ella-Jayne in his arms.

"I have breakfast ready for you. You'll eat, then sleep," Faye said, surprising Pepper by the firmness of her voice.

"Yes, ma'am. But I've got phone calls to make."

"Food, then you can call. That cousin of yours was definitely born under a troubled sign."

"Trouble sign," EllaJayne agreed and patted AJ's face. His eyes closed for a brief moment as he pulled her tighter to him.

PEPPER HAD MADE herself stay out in the garden for an hour. When she'd finally come in, AJ looked even worse—dark circles under his eyes and his face gray-white instead of the usual healthy tan. Faye had already told her that he'd eaten nothing, but drunk a full pot of coffee and been on the phone non-stop.

"What's up?" she asked casually when she came into the kitchen.

"This is how it is," he started, staring hard at his inky cup of coffee. "EllaJayne's mama has two good legs to stand on for what she and Nevin are saying, according to my attorney from back home. He helped me come up with the agreement, which isn't worth the paper it's written on, apparently. Guess he wasn't much of an attorney." He took a slug of coffee. "He told me to not fight her about custody until I pay her off, then get the papers signed, sealed and delivered."

"You can't turn that little girl over to a woman who'd…sell her," Pepper said, keeping her voice low. Faye had EllaJayne in the living room, playing with the plastic ranch kit AJ had brought with him.

"No choice. This is short-term pain for long-term gain."

"This is a child we're talking about."

"I know that." He stood abruptly, the chair skittering away. Butch moved quickly, aware as Pepper was that AJ was volatile, and could lose it at any second. She wasn't afraid of him. She was afraid *for* him.

"Let me call Lavonda's brother-in-law. He's an Arizona attorney. We're in Arizona. Or what about Chief Rudy? He'd send your cousin and that woman—" she couldn't believe how angry she was at AJ's ex "—scurrying back under their rock."

"If I get the law involved, it might not just be my custody that we'd lose."

We? What did he mean? "What more can there be than custody? The money?"

AJ rubbed again at his nape.

"What else is there?" she whispered to him.

He pulled away and kept his back to her, like he couldn't face her.

"The shyster attorney Nevin got for Suzy says if I don't hand over Baby Girl—" his voice wavered just enough that she could hear his heart breaking

"—they'll…have me arrested for kidnapping. They're saying I didn't have custody, so I had no right to take her from Kentucky."

"He's your cousin… She didn't want—"

He turned to her and his storm-gray eyes were flat and dark. She wanted to pull him back into her arms.

"I'll get this place on the market. Bobby Ames will take care of that. I'll go back to Kentucky and fight it there, but I have to let them take EllaJayne."

"You can't."

"I'll get her back. I'll be right there. I'll move in with Suzy."

"What?"

"It's simple. I'll go with my baby's mama until I can get the money. That's all they want. The money."

"AJ, we can fight this."

"There is no we."

"But you just said—" she stopped herself. They'd knocked boots, but they hadn't made any promises. They certainly hadn't said the L word. *Words don't matter much when the heart's involved*, Daddy Gene's voice echoed in her head. She couldn't let AJ walk away like this. "Of course there's a we. We've been living together and caring for your daughter. You've been helping me make the Angel Crossing Community Garden a reality. We've been sharing a bed."

"We shared a bed once, and I was stuck here until the estate settled."

"You could have stayed with Danny. You could have done a hundred other things."

"This was easy," he said. His mouth had pulled into a grim line. "I'm leaving. I was always leaving.

I don't know what kind of fantasy life you've built for us. I was never staying."

"Maybe that was true before—"

"I slept with you? You were here. I'm a man. That's all it was."

"Go. Go now." Her voice barely pushed past the knot of pain in her throat. How could she not have seen that he didn't care, that it was all about the sex? She was a grown woman, not a girl. Dear Lord, this hurt.

"That's what I've been saying."

Finally, he walked away, his cowboy stroll less confident, more hesitant. She didn't care if he'd hurt himself again. Why would she care?

"You're not taking that baby with you," she shouted after him. He didn't stop. She watched him walk away from her and understood that today was officially the worst day of her life.

"You're just going to let your ass of a cousin take your kid and your ranch?" Danny asked AJ while they sipped beer at his apartment.

"I'm regrouping." AJ really wished he could get drunk. Wasn't happening, though, because just a sip of beer was trying to crawl back up his throat.

"That's what it looks like. Your daughter is out at Santa Faye Ranch. You're here and your slimy cousin is staying at the motor court."

AJ slammed down the beer bottle. Didn't anyone in Angel Crossing understand? None of this was what he wanted to do. It was this or put the final nail into Pepper's life. He'd inherited her ranch, and now his cousin was threatening her career. He'd refused to say anything to her earlier. He couldn't add that to her burdens. He'd take care of it by going back to Kentucky, paying the money and getting all this straightened out. Then he'd stay far away from Arizona because he'd guess after all this, Pepper would never want to see him again. He got up from his chair and paced around the small apartment.

Danny squinted at AJ as he sipped his own beer. "Finally got your mad on. Thought you were going to spend the whole night moping."

"I'm not moping."

"Coulda fooled me."

"I gave Nevin two days to produce the paperwork. Then I'm going back home to fight it out there. Pepper and her job will be safe." AJ shut up. He'd not meant to say anything about Pepper.

"What about her job?" Danny's blue eyes were cold and fierce.

"Well, hell." AJ picked up the beer again to have something to do with his hands.

"Tell me now. Or I'm getting the chief involved. I'll tell him that your cousin threatened Pepper, which it sounds like he did?"

"He's making noise that he and Suzy will tell the authorities Pepper knew that I had my daughter illegally and she didn't report it to the authorities. It could mean her losing her license to practice medicine."

"Shit, man," Danny said. "Why didn't you tell me? I *will* call Rudy and have him go out and arrest that piss-ant."

"I'm taking care of it by going back to Kentucky and selling the ranch, then no one will need to deal with me again."

"Not the way it works in Angel Crossing."

"What do you mean?"

"Your cousin threatened not only your daughter but also Pepper. I've already told you that's not allowed."

"What are you talking about? This is my problem."

"This is Angel Crossing."

"I know where I am."

"Sit down and let me tell you what's going to happen. What's already happening." Danny pointed to the hard wooden kitchen chair. AJ dropped into it, suddenly exhausted.

"Everyone knows it's BS what your cousin is saying about 'kidnapping' your daughter, then 'abandoning' her. You know how family is. Well, maybe you don't, but in a family, you can say anything about your siblings or your crazy great-aunt. The minute someone not family says a word, you close ranks and are ready to kick butt and take names."

"What does that have to do with Angel Crossing? They want me to kick Nevin's ass?"

"Maybe. What I meant was that Angel Crossing might say things about Faye and Pepper but they're family. No one else can say things about them."

"Makes no sense."

Danny held up his beer bottle in salute. "Welcome to town, son."

AJ sort of followed what Danny was saying, but it didn't matter. He feared Nevin might actually have the law on his side.

Danny tried again, "I see you're still confused. Bobby Ames was working on the attorneys in Kentucky before he went to his Stuff and Display Conference. Chief Rudy's already talking to the law. Claudette at the clinic is making calls and sending emails. Apparently, the twins at Jim's refused to serve Nevin, said that he was 'visibly intoxicated' when he walked into the bar."

"Was he?"

"Nah. They were just messing with him because he messed with Faye and Pepper."

"It's my problem. My daughter. My ex."

"You've been adopted. Gene vouched for you even before he died. Leaving you the ranch means that you're a stand-up cowboy. Pillar-of-the-community kind of guy. Who'da thought it, huh? Considering us, back in the day."

"Jeez. This is crazy. I can't stay. Nevin isn't smart but he's clever. He's not kidding that he'll try to get Pepper's license revoked. It'll be better for her if I go back to Kentucky. Nevin will follow me. I don't even need to be here to sell the ranch. I can do all of that remotely."

"What about your daughter?"

"I'm doing this for her as much as for Pepper." Right now, she was with the Bourne family, including Butch—her favorite people. AJ had made his way onto her list, but taking her back to Kentucky... He didn't have a choice if the papers said what Nevin insisted they did. He'd do what the order said. Breaking the law and him getting thrown in jail wouldn't protect Baby Girl. He was fighting for her no matter what Danny or anyone else thought. And what did Pepper think? He was a coward? That really hurt. He took a slug of beer. Everything had been so easy before he'd met his daughter. He wouldn't change it, though. Life without her…he couldn't imagine it. Then he'd met Pepper and everything— "Sheep tails," he said out loud.

"What finally made it through that thick skull? That I'm right?"

He wasn't sure he could say it. His tongue had gone numb as the truth smacked him between the eyes, ringing his bell as hard as Twister II, the high-money bull of the 2010 season. "I love Pepper," he said thickly, his tongue too big for his mouth.

"Of course you do, you idiot. Everyone knows that. That's the real reason they like you."

"CLAUDETTE, WHO'S NEXT?" Pepper asked, hoping for a long, complicated case with a crotchety old cowboy. She wanted a distraction and someone to vent her annoyance on, no matter if that was unfair.

"*You're* next, missy," her assistant said. "We've organized an intervention."

"Very funny. I know I've been hitting the Fiddle Faddle pretty hard, but I don't think I've gotten to intervention level."

"We're done with appointments for today and Devil's Food reserved us the meeting room. Lavonda wanted to call it the war room. Faye said no."

Pepper froze. What exactly was going on? She'd assumed Claudette had been speaking figuratively. "Faye? Lavonda?"

"Yes. Grammy Marie, too. EllaJayne is going to be hanging with Chief Rudy. He's hankering for grandkids, so he wants a dry run. We're out of here." Claudette shooed Pepper down the sidewalk and into Devil's Food.

As Pepper walked through the diner, she got looks of sympathy and a couple of encouraging nods. Danny waved to her from his stool. "He's not here," he told her. "I'm working on it, though."

What did that mean? Pepper tried to stop her momentum. Claudette gave her a poke. Pepper jumped forward through the door to a small side room with one large table, which was used as a meeting room.

Faye drifted out of her seat and enveloped Pepper. The patchouli and baby powder scent comforted her for a moment. Then Pepper looked at the filled chairs and the determined looks on all the women's faces. It really was an intervention.

"Sit," her mother said as she directed Pepper to the head of the long table. "We need to re-align your—"

"It's an intervention. We decided," Grammy Marie said.

Lavonda with her sleek hair and large dark eyes stood and immediately commanded the room. "Whatever we call it doesn't matter. What matters is saving that precious little girl and getting Pepper her—"

"Her destiny," Faye said.

Lavonda just smiled. "Again, the labels are less important than the actions, and we've got a lot of actions to organize. Danny said AJ will get his paperwork from Nevin tomorrow, which doesn't give us much time to straighten everything out, including making sure that Kentucky yahoo doesn't get your license taken away."

"What?" Pepper breathed.

"Now, don't get mad at AJ," Grammy Marie said. "Nevin threatened to go to the authorities about you to get your license pulled."

"Why didn't he say anything to me? Nevin couldn't do that—" Pepper stopped, knowing Nevin might have been able to get her in trouble. But could she think about AJ's silence?

Faye said, "Gene was the same way. He'd think I was too delicate to face the ugly parts of life. But I wasn't. We're not." She smiled at her daughter.

"Of course she's not," Lavonda said. "Danny told us and I added that to the list of items that Spence, my lawyer brother-in-law, and the chief needed to address. Nevin had some hopped-up charge that you should have reported EllaJayne as kidnapped. Danny's getting a copy of the document so we have all the details. Spence said he'd check it out. We'd have asked Bobby Ames, but he's at a taxidermy conference in Oregon. But I called him and he said Spence would have been his choice if we'd asked him."

Pepper wasn't certain exactly what was going on. AJ had been protecting her even as he planned to leave her and take his daughter with him. She needed to stay focused on what was important: AJ getting custody of his daughter. Knowing he needed the money for that had made her less hurt that Daddy Gene had left the ranch to him. It had all worked out for the best.

"I see you thinking through this," Faye said. "Don't use your brain. Use your heart. You're so good at that. That's why you work at the clinic and why you're starting the gardens. You've got such a huge heart." Faye's voice had a tender edge to it.

"I'm just confused what we're doing here," Pepper said. "If it's to help EllaJayne and you need me to sign something for the attorney, Lavonda, just let me know. Otherwise—"

"Later. We may need that signature," Lavonda said. "But that's not what this is about."

Pepper looked at the women. Some were patients and all were friends.

Grammy Marie stared right at Pepper and said, "You're in love with EllaJayne, because who wouldn't be, but more importantly, you're in love with AJ."

"I don't think so," Pepper said but with the words hanging in the air, her answer wasn't as sure as she would have liked.

"Grammy Marie, we decided that wasn't what we were doing today," Lavonda said patiently.

"She's right," Faye said. "Marie's right, I mean. It's as obvious as the nose on my face. Pepper has to come to that conclusion on her own. We shouldn't be pushing her."

The room erupted, the women talking over each other in their enthusiasm. The passionate faces around the table made Pepper warm and fuzzy inside, just like when she got a hug from a patient. Not like her and AJ. That was volcano and silk. She certainly wanted him. So what? She wanted a lot of things in life that she couldn't have. Plus, she had more than enough with her patients and the garden project. Then she remembered her and AJ together. It wasn't just burning up the sheets that came to mind. She also felt in her heart the nights they spent in the garden together with Butch and EllaJayne, even the meals with Faye.

"Lordy be," Pepper said. The room got silent.

"She figured it out," Faye said. "Good girl. I knew you could do it on your own. I told them."

"AJ's made it clear he's moving along, and I'm not leaving Angel Crossing. This is my home."

"Of course you're not leaving Angel Crossing or Santa Faye Ranch," her mother said.

"We can't stay at the ranch and AJ…that's clear, too. I'm in infatuation."

"No. You're not, plus it can work," Lavonda said. "My sister did a long-distance thing. And look at Jones and me. He wasn't going to stay in Arizona, but here we are. The good thing about life is that it changes."

Grammy Marie chimed in, "Love conquers all."

Faye fluttered over to Pepper and took her hands while the room quieted again. "You know what to do. That's one of your gifts. You can see clearly the path that you need to take, even if it's tough. You do it with compassion and caring, but you always know. So what do you know about AJ? That you love him. He loves you. He has to clear up his past and you'll help him with that. What else do you need to know?"

"How exactly this can work? And how exactly I can be sure that AJ cares for me? Or even that I really care for him?"

"That's easy, sweetie. You love him because he loves your dog, my Beauties, his daughter and Santa Faye Ranch. Of course he loves you. Why else would a cowboy take up farming and herding walking yarn balls?"

Chapter Sixteen

"What did you want, Danny?" AJ asked as he walked into his friend's office. He stopped when he saw Pepper sitting there. His breath got gummed up in his throat. He reached out his hand before he could stop himself but let it drop without touching her. Didn't matter if he loved her. His life was crap right now and he couldn't drag her into that. "Pepper," he said, nodding to her and pulling off his hat. He didn't take the chair next to her. He'd be too close.

"Good," Danny said. "Sit."

"No. You're busy—"

"We were waiting for you."

AJ looked hard at his friend, trying to understand what he wanted and why he was involving him. The plan was already in motion. He'd meet Nevin, see the papers, then go back to Kentucky with EllaJayne.

"AJ, sit. This might take a little while," Pepper said. He couldn't look at her because he might just break down. He kept his gaze on Danny and sat.

"What did you two want?" AJ asked.

Danny gave a politician's smile. It looked as genuine as Dolly Parton's...hair. "Pepper and I spoke with Spencer...my sister's brother-in-law. He's a good attorney. He and Lavonda actually came up with this. I hate to say that my sister had a good idea, but there it is."

"You going to get to the point sometime this century?" Sitting this close to Pepper had AJ thinking about those few precious nights together and how giving up on ever being with her like that again was like breathing underwater. Impossible.

"I want you to understand that this isn't an off-the-cuff idea, you blockhead. We only had two days, but we've made it work. So when you go see Nevin this afternoon…yes, everyone knows you're meeting with him…you can present him with this, and the chief will go with you. Yes. He will because he doesn't want any trouble. And I know you, AJ. There could be trouble when your Kentucky cousins are involved. They're like a pack of jackals."

"Get to the point, Danforth," AJ said, glaring at the man who used to be his pal. The lemon and clove scent of Pepper surrounded him, weaving its way through his scrambled brain.

"Danforth?" Pepper asked. "Really?"

"Family name," Danny said with another politician's smile. "I want to make sure you understand, AJ. All of Angel Crossing helped with this plan and will benefit from it, including Pepper and Faye. We take this very seriously. You understand?"

Did he? He didn't really believe that the town had adopted him. He'd never felt like that before. He'd lived in Pinetown his entire life and people wouldn't spit on him if he were on fire.

"I'll take the silence as understanding," Danny said. "We have a grant from the state that is earmarked for the Angel Crossing Community Garden Project."

AJ finally turned to Pepper. "You got the money. Why didn't you tell me?"

"You're leaving."

That about said it all. She didn't look like she cared for him. Danny had been wrong. "Congratulations."

"Yeah, yeah, yeah. Hooray," Danny said. "What that means is that we have money, which Angel Crossing never has."

None of this mattered. AJ was leaving. He had to clear up things in Kentucky, which he guessed, knowing his luck, would go as smoothly as concrete through a straw. It was just he'd changed so much in such a short time, it was hard to remember that AJ. Knowing about his little girl and then seeing her for the first time…he'd known right then life would never be the same. Exactly like when he'd seen Pepper in the flesh.

"Put us both out of our misery," she said. AJ turned to her and saw the pain on her face. He wanted to pull her into his arms. He stood up and leaned across Danny's desk.

"Stop beating around the damned bush and just tell us."

"Sit down, AJ. I'm getting there. I'm not dragging this out. I really need both of you to understand what's at stake."

"Are you saying there's a chance that the grant will go away?" Pepper asked. "What's that got to do with AJ?"

"Fine. I spent at least fifteen minutes on my speech but you two are ruining it. The council and I met.

Then the ladies from Devil's Food talked with me. You know who I mean, Pepper." AJ was surprised when she blushed. "We believe the best use for the grant is not to buy equipment and the empty lots in town. The grant will be a down payment, along with the collection that came together from Angel Crossing, to buy Santa Faye Ranch from AJ."

AJ looked at Pepper to gauge her reaction to her grant being hijacked by him and his problems. She looked...happy. She smiled at him, tears shining in her eyes and her smile wobbly at the corners. "Why didn't they tell me? This is a great solution."

"Good thing you think so because it's a done deal. We didn't want to wait. Afraid if Nevin got wind of this, he'd find some way to mess it up. He's smart like a fox."

AJ wasn't listening to Danny. His gaze hadn't left Pepper's face. Dear Lord. She *did* love him. He could see it in her eyes. He pulled her from the chair and into his embrace. "Thank you. Thank you. I didn't think I could love you more than I did, but now I do."

"You love me?" she asked with wonder, leaning back enough to look directly into his eyes. "Thank God. You love me. I love you, too. I love you enough to...well, I would have let you go if that was the best thing. You know that whole 'if you love something, leave it go' nonsense."

He pulled her close again and said into her ear. "I'm never leaving you go."

"But you don't want to stay in Arizona. You said that—"

He kissed her and she kissed him back with her whole heart.

"YOU'RE THINKING TOO LOUDLY," AJ said as he squeezed Pepper's hand where it lay between them on the bench seat of his pickup. "It will all work out."

"Later I want to talk with you about what Nevin threatened me with and you not telling me. Right now, I'm just trying to take in the fact that you aren't on your way out of town. I had prepared myself for that. Instead we're... What are we?"

"Not sure. Not worried."

He was right. What did it matter? They knew they loved each other. They'd said it right there in the mayor's office. About as official as you could get. Now, they were going to save AJ and his little girl. And then what?

"You're doing it again. We'll worry about tomorrow, tomorrow."

"That sounds like something from a fortune cookie. What if this—" she waved her hand at them "—is just physical?"

"You really believe that?" he glanced away from the road and smiled that special cowboy grin.

"It could be."

"I don't think so. I pulled weeds for you. I haven't done that since my mama threatened me with no dinner."

"You were just trying to get me horizontal by impressing me with your green thumb."

"Could be. But I want to stay here and keep pulling weeds and plowing and growing good food for good people."

Her chest tightened and her eyes stung. He got it. Got her. "I love you."

"Well, duh," he said and laughed, before pulling

her hand to his mouth and gently kissing the knuckles. "Now, stop distracting me. You don't want me to drive into a ditch."

She allowed herself to float in the sparkly bright love. The next few hours wouldn't be so sparkly bright. She was going to enjoy this little bit of time alone. They were driving to the ranch to meet up with Nevin, as well as Danny, half of the town council, and half of the women from the Devil's Food Diner Back Room Mafia—a name invented by Chief Rudy. Faye said that once everyone heard what would be happening between AJ and his cousin, they insisted on coming out as witnesses, moral support or muscle, in the case of one or two of her cowboy patients. They were going to get Nevin to sign the paper or else. Taking care of people didn't mean she had to do it all herself. When had she thought it was her exclusive job to save the world? And when had she become so arrogant she thought she could?

"You're doing it again. Tell me what you want to plant and what kind of chickens you fancy?"

She pulled in a breath and turned her brain to the question, allowing herself to think about the new life that would be hers. Not exactly the one she'd planned, but that was good, too. She wouldn't be alone to face her problems. There was everyone from Angel Crossing and even Faye. She turned to smile at AJ. He'd be there today, and she was pretty sure that might be all she needed for the rest of her life.

"WHAT THE HELL is this?" AJ's cousin Nevin asked after strolling potbelly first from his pickup with Kentucky plates and twenty years of dirt and rust. "Do they know what you done?"

AJ moved forward, and Pepper stayed glued to his side. Chief Rudy stepped in. "This is Angel Crossing, and we look after our own. These are our own."

Nevin's washed-out blue eyes were nearly hidden by bangs of thinning dirty-blond hair. "I'm here to settle personal business with my cousin."

The chief spoke before Pepper or AJ could open their mouths. "Whatever business you have to transact with AJ, you'll do here in the open."

"Fine. Then you can all hear what kind of man he is, stealing that there baby from its mama."

"He did not," Pepper said, surprising herself with her own vehemence. "He saved that baby. He sacrificed—"

"Nevin," AJ broke in and walked around the chief to stand squarely in front of his cousin. There was no resemblance at all, even with both of them in jeans, boots and T-shirts. "You and Suzy want money. I've got money. You just need to sign this." AJ whipped out the paperwork and the assistant for the police department came forward. She would notarize the document on the spot. They weren't leaving anything to chance. There was at least one smartphone filming the entire exchange.

Nevin looked down at the papers. "That's not enough. I talked to people who know what our cousin Gene left you."

"This is all you and Suzy will get. I think the courts frown on blackmail. Don't they, chief?" AJ didn't take his eyes from Nevin.

"That's right. We take threats like that very seriously."

"Do ya now?" Nevin asked, looking around the crowd before his nasty gaze landed on Pepper. "You're his piece, huh?"

AJ reached forward and grabbed the front of his cousin's Hell Raiser, Hay Maker T-shirt, bunching it in his fist. "Shut up and sign the paper."

She waited for Chief Rudy to step forward and stop AJ. When the chief didn't move a muscle, Pepper started toward the men. Her mother held tight to her, whispering in her ear, "You've got to let your man be a man."

What did that mean? She couldn't let him get beat up, not for her, not for the ranch. Except this wasn't her fight. This was AJ's. This was about his baby. For EllaJayne she would do the same thing. She didn't struggle, carefully sizing up Nevin. AJ could definitely take him in a fair fight but fair didn't seem to be in his cousin's vocabulary.

"Don't you see what he's doing?" Nevin squealed. "Arrest him."

Chief Rudy turned away.

"Sign the damned paper," AJ said again, his voice low and menacing.

"It's not enough, cuz. We've got expenses."

"Sign the paper. What's in there—that's all you're ever getting from me." AJ's fist tightened in the thin T-shirt material while sweat beaded Nevin's pasty face.

In the silence, Nevin's breathing rasped. Heat beat down on Pepper's head. No one moved. Every eye was on the men.

"Boot," EllaJayne yelled from the house as the dog bolted across the yard and into the crowd. The toddler followed on his heels, snatched up by Faye. Butch stopped at AJ's side and growled at Nevin, hackles raised. Pepper gaped at her poodle of a shepherd. She'd never heard that noise before, low and threatening.

"Get that dog away," Nevin said, kicking out his foot and hitting Butch squarely on the nose, knocking him to the ground where the dog lay stunned. Pepper raced forward and saw Nevin's feet leave the ground as the crowd yelled.

"That's it," Chief Rudy said. "We've given you a chance to be a man about this, but kicking a dog… what kind of man does that? No man at all. Let him go, AJ, he's under arrest for animal cruelty."

A murmur of approval went through the group as Nevin protested and Butch stood, shaking his head a little in confusion. His butt started wagging and he took three steps and sat on AJ's feet.

Pepper looked at her cowboy, his face stiff with disgust and anger. His storm-gray gaze stayed on his cousin and his grip didn't loosen. She went to him.

"You can release him now. The chief will arrest him, and Butch is fine. We're fine. He'll sign. We're giving them money, and it's more than they deserve. How can he and Suzy refuse? They should just take the money and run." She turned to Nevin using the same stare she used on cowboys when they came to the clinic. "He knows what the score is. It's like the sheriff said: Angel Crossing looks after its own, and we're its own."

"He and Suzy don't deserve a dime," AJ ground out.

"Maybe not, but if it makes sure EllaJayne is yours forever, without strings and without a mama who only sees dollar signs, then it's money more than well spent. Plus, you don't have a choice," she said and then rose on her toes to speak directly in his ear, "We all decided to spend our money this way. If you don't sign, what will that mean to Angel Crossing Community Garden?"

He turned and his face relaxed a tiny bit. "I should have known this was about your veggies." His hand loosened. "He's all yours, chief."

Pepper pulled AJ into her arms and the cluster of friends and neighbors clapped as she kissed him hard on the mouth.

AJ JUST STOPPED himself from pulling Pepper closer by the butt. "I love you," he said, not feeling silly or scared. It all felt right. He could barely remember the cowboy he'd been, the one who'd gone from woman to woman looking for…well, for what he had now. Family. Friends. Home. Lordy be, as Pepper said. His eyes burned with tears.

"Boot, Boot," EllaJayne yelled. He and Pepper broke apart. He scooped up Baby Girl. His finally. No more Suzy. The mother who didn't want this gorgeous human. A part of him was sad for that. Another selfish part was grateful because it meant that she was all his. No. Not just his. His and Pepper's. His chest started to burn along with his eyes. Lordy be.

He pulled Pepper back to him, squashing his daughter between them and loving all of it, even the scrabbling of Butch's claws on his leg and his daughter's screams for her favorite playmate. His little girl needed a brother or a sister…whoa, cowboy.

He'd barely gotten a grasp on being a daddy and on knowing he loved Pepper. Now he was imagining new babies. He pulled them all closer before letting them go enough so Pepper could stand beside him as they faced the small crowd. How did he thank this town that had accepted him as one of their own?

"Wait," Faye said before he could open his mouth. "Gene would be so proud. So happy." The tears in her voice were clear, but she smiled.

AJ tightened his grip on Pepper, knowing mention of Gene would make her a little sad. The wound of his passing, the only father she'd known, had not completely healed.

"He certainly would be," AJ said when Faye didn't continue. "I know he loved this town. I know that because he told me. Gene was the greatest cowboy I knew. Not because he won buckles or was in the money. He was the best because he shared his knowledge and his six-pack, when needed, for purely medicinal purposes, of course." He paused for the knowing laughter, then went on, "I'm not certain why he left me his ranch, but I will be forever grateful because it got me my daughter and—" He stopped himself, uncertain he was ready to share exactly what he felt for Pepper.

"Oh, man, just kiss her again," Danny said.

The crowd shouted and he did kiss her again. A light promise of more to come.

"This is just what Gene wanted," Faye said when things quieted.

"What do you mean?" Pepper asked, stepping away from AJ and staring down her mother.

"Sweetie, you know Gene loved you, and he knew

he wouldn't be on this earth forever." Faye hesitated and her voice quavered when she went on. "He was so sure AJ was the cowboy for you."

Now, AJ wondered what exactly Faye was getting at.

Faye said, "We discussed it. So, Gene decided… sweetie, he just wanted you to be happy. And when I saw AJ and his baby, I knew Gene had been right."

"You're saying he set us up?" Pepper asked sounding as gut-punched shocked as AJ.

"Why else wouldn't he leave the ranch to us?"

"Faye, he didn't do that. He left it to AJ because he saved Daddy Gene from that bull."

"He certainly was grateful but that debt was paid to AJ in the hundreds of ways he helped him over the years at the rodeo and by checking in with him even after he left. This was about you, sweetie. He wanted to make sure you were cared for."

AJ could think of a lot of reasons that had nothing to do with matchmaking. The sparks of heat from Pepper told AJ she might be ready to explode with all that anger directed at her mother, which would lead to a lot of words Pepper couldn't take back and would regret for a long time. "Faye," he said loudly, catching everyone's attention. "Gene knew his stuff. But," he said emphatically because this was important to him, "Pepper can take care of herself and does it with empathy and style. She's cared for you and for this town because that's what she does. She didn't need Gene to find anyone to care for her. But I'm grateful he did because I can't imagine my life without her." He finally looked at Pepper and had to look away so the burning in his eyes didn't turn into tears. "I'm grateful he brought me to Angel Crossing because there's no place on this earth I'd rather be. Or where there are better folks."

Chapter Seventeen

AJ stood with his dusty booted foot on the lowest rung of the corral. Another time in his life, there would have been bulls or horses on the other side of the fence. Not in his new life. No. Here was a milling herd of furballs. Alpacas and llamas. He shook his head, amazed at the turns his life had taken. He couldn't even be upset that Gene had a lot to do with those curves because he'd ended up with Pepper and EllaJayne. No regrets in either case. Maybe one small regret that EllaJayne's mama wouldn't know her wonderful daughter. Some women just weren't cut out to be mamas.

"I could hear you stewing from the house," Pepper said.

He turned and smiled because, well, he was happy as a bull in a field of heifers. Well, one heifer and he was a smart enough cowboy to not share that thought. "Not stewing," he said to her. "Thinking about how lucky I am."

"You think you're getting lucky tonight?" she asked with a secret smile as she walked up to him and snuggled into his side, despite the lingering heat of the day.

"I didn't think tonight would be about luck. Thought that was a sure thing." She poked him in the ribs. He laughed. "I meant lucky that Gene decided to play matchmaker. Lucky Suzy would take money over motherhood. And, luckiest of all? That Angel Crossing is allowing us to rent to own Santa Faye Ranch."

"I don't know if I believe Daddy Gene had any plans for you and me," Pepper said seriously. "I'm just going to say EllaJayne couldn't have a better daddy than you, and Suzy is going to miss out on knowing an awesome person. But I hope if she ever changes her mind on wanting to see her daughter, you'll think about it."

"She doesn't deserve—"

"It's not what Suzy deserves. It's what EllaJayne might want and need."

He squeezed her hard because that was Pepper. Thinking about others. "You're right, of course."

"I like the sound of that." She squeezed him close, then said with a hint of jealousy and humor, "One day I'll want to hear all about your sordid past. But not tonight."

"Good. It's a lot less sordid and a lot more ordinary than you think." They stood arm in arm watching the furballs find a comfortable place to settle. Faye and EllaJayne were spending the night with Grammy Marie. He'd cut off Faye when she'd tried to give him advice on how to spend the evening.

"Faye told me that our astrological charts indicate we will make beautiful babies," Pepper said.

"I don't know if I'll ever get used to her…how she… Aw, hell…let's go to bed." He didn't want to think about the future. All he wanted to focus on was Pepper and letting her know again how much he loved her. She pressed her soft breasts against him as she pulled his head down for a kiss, saying softly, "Bed. My favorite three-letter word."

Pepper's lips were petal-soft under his. When had he gotten addicted to them, and to her? He lifted her against him, wanting her supple heat. He deepened the kiss until both of their breaths jerked in and out.

He pulled away, slowly, reluctantly. "I love you."

"I love you, too," she said, cupping his face, her brown gaze locked on him, shining. His chest swelled. He gave her a quick kiss, then pulled her toward the house, his feet moving faster and faster. Pepper's laughter rang out as they ran into the house, landing on her bed with a bounce.

He wanted her now and he knew he'd want her in ten years…twenty, fifty. That was heady stuff. He took her lips and his hand loved her curves as he quickly stripped her. When he got down to her plain white panties and bra, he thought they were sexier than any lace and silk. They made what was under them a mystery that he needed to discover. He buried his face between her breasts, his hand slipping into the cup of her bra to tease her nipple "Yes," she gasped, her hands holding his head in place as she moved under his lips. Her responsiveness sparked his own scalding need.

AJ's mouth tasted the sweet skin as his hands slipped her bra from her breasts. When he shifted for a moment, Pepper shuddered and whispered, "You have too many clothes on." Then she wriggled out from under him. Her hands, small and competent, opened the snaps on his shirt and pushed it off in one motion. She went for his jeans and he reached for her, clasping her butt and making her jump. He wanted her to hurry or this would all end before it had even started.

"I want you naked and I want you on that bed," she said, her voice rough. She bent over to take off his boots. As she shook her fanny at him, a deep-from-the-gut groan broke from behind his clenched teeth. She had to know the sexy power she had over him.

She stood and turned. "Your pants. Take them off. No, wait," she said, a gleam in her eyes that made him wish he had a whole case of condoms. "That's my treat." She brushed her fingers along his shuddering abs, dipping her fingers under his waistband before opening the metal button. He reversed their positions, kissing her while he stripped her and him of the final barriers of their clothing. No more teasing. He fumbled his condom on and slid into her. Finding a thrill and contentment that he hadn't known he'd been chasing.

"I love you," she said, holding him still for a moment before moving her hips and sending them both flying.

"I love you," he whispered as he tucked her already familiar curves against his body. They were both where they needed to be now and forever.

AJ LOOKED OUT over the dusty parking lot filled with pop-up canopies and plastic tables. He refused to panic. His daughter was here somewhere. He could find her. She hadn't done a disappearing act like this in a while. He looked over the large lot that had been empty just yesterday. Today was a big party, where the town was celebrating the weekly farmers market, planting for the new year and the second grant they'd gotten from a big foundation that understood Pepper's vision.

Darn it. Where was his daughter? Where was Pepper, who was wearing a bright lime-green hat today. She said it was easier to see her, plus her mother had given it to her for luck with the new planting season. Faye had told him it was to increase their fertility. EllaJayne was enough for them right now, thank you very much.

"You missing something, cowboy?" Chief Rudy asked, catching AJ off guard.

"Not missing, exactly."

The older man squinted at him from under the brim of his cowboy hat. "They're over there by the mayor's tent." He gestured with his chin.

AJ nodded and headed that way. He got waylaid twice by members of the Community Garden. He hurried on and managed to avoid the ladies who used the furballs' fleece. They were trying to convince him the spinners and knitters needed Santa Faye Ranch to get "just one or two angora goats." That's what they'd said when they'd talked him into increasing the number of alpacas—two more in a buff color, which turned into six because otherwise they would've been put down. He'd told them firmly they were not running an alpaca rescue group.

AJ checked at the mayor's tent, but Danny said he hadn't seen Pepper or EllaJayne for at least twenty minutes. AJ scanned the crowd again, looking for

Pepper and his daughter. Soon to be *their* daughter. The adoption process was nearly complete.

Where the heck were they? He got stopped a dozen more times, turning down tastes of dishes being created for the Best Potluck contest. Everyone had just seen Pepper. Finally, he got pointed in the direction of the old movie house that hadn't been in operation since the 1970s and hadn't been grand even in its heyday. Everyone had been wondering how much longer it would stand. That sort of headache was for his friend Danny. AJ had his work cut out for him at Santa Faye Ranch, running herd on the furballs and setting up a website, Lord save them all. Pepper still worked at the clinic because she loved it and the town needed her. That meant the running of the garden had fallen to him and Faye, who was surprisingly sharp when it came to the farm. Of course, she'd grown up in a commune. She knew how to get people to work for free. She was organizing tonight's feast, even though it included meat. She said next time they would do an all-vegetarian potluck. He didn't think the meat-eating residents would go for that, but he was learning Faye could accomplish anything.

He heard Butch barking. EllaJayne couldn't be far behind. The two of them were attached at the hip. She still called him Boot, even though her nearly three-year-old vocabulary had gotten so much better. "Baby Girl," he shouted. "Butch. Come here now." He waited for an answer. Nothing. Darn it. He might just have to go back and ask the chief for help finding—there they were. EllaJayne was walking down the sidewalk toward the old theater with Butch keeping watch at her side. Where was Pepper?

EllaJayne screeched in joy. He followed the sound into the abandoned movie theater. Great. Creepy old theater with rats and who knew what else.

"Baby Girl," he yelled, as he walked in, blinking when he noticed it wasn't dark.

"Darn it, EllaJayne," Pepper said. "You were supposed to stay with Grammy Marie."

"Oops," his daughter said, her new word for getting out of any mischief.

"Pepper," he said.

She turned around, looking even guiltier than his daughter and the dog. The three of them stood in the theater's lobby, lit well from a duo of chandeliers.

"I was going to surprise you."

"Surprise me?"

"Danny found an angel donor and more money from somewhere—he's a genius with that. We—Angel Crossing, I mean—bought the theater. We're going to turn it into a permanent, undercover Farmers Market for our extra produce and for the urban gardens in town and for all the items the ladies make from the furballs. It'll take a year or so, but won't it be great?"

He could see how much work it would be. He'd trust her on this, but he figured it'd take much more than a year.

He hugged her. "'Great' might not be what I'm saying in a couple of months. Who'll be running this project?" She was quiet and he got suspicious. "No. I already have the new fields laid out and the chickens ordered."

"Chickens? You got me chickens?" She kissed him hard.

A year and a half ago he'd never have imagined a

passel of hens would get him a lip-lock. He squeezed her butt for good measure. "That was supposed to be my surprise for…later," he said quietly with a waggle of his brows.

"You thought laying hens would get *you* laid," Pepper whispered for his ears only. "You do know your woman." She gave him another deep kiss.

He liked the sound of that. He wished he could thank his cousin for his matchmaking. *Damn right, and you'd better do right by her*, Gene's voice rang out in his head.

"What?" Pepper asked at his expression. "I know the theater's a lot to take in." She turned and gave the narrow, dusty space a loving look, exactly like the one she used on the fields of beans and kale.

"I'm just trying to figure out how you turned a cowboy into a farmer," he answered.

"*S-e-x.*"

He laughed until he heard Baby Girl singing, "*S-e-x. S-e-x. S-e-x.*"

"You're going to explain that to Grammy Marie."

"No problem. I'll just tell her it's Grana Faye's fault." Now, his daughter added Faye's name to her chant.

He held Pepper again in his arms and watched his daughter move little piles of nuts and bolts around the lobby, while Butch trailed behind her. In these kinds of moments, he realized he was happy, beyond happy. He wasn't sure exactly when that had happened. He knew it would last until the next time the furballs got out, but he couldn't imagine his life any other way.

"You told him," Faye said from where she stood at the entrance to the small old-fashioned theater.

"She told me," he answered, not moving away from Pepper. "But she still hasn't told me who will be running the project." He tried to sound stern.

"Me and you, of course," Faye said. "I'm a water sign."

"Of course. Makes total sense." It did in some weird Faye way. "When will you start?"

"The mayor and I are discussing that. I need to cleanse the building, then we'll be ready. We have great plans. Gene would be so happy." Faye's smile wavered a little. She still obviously missed him.

Pepper pulled away from him and went to her mother. "He would. He'd like what you've helped us do at the ranch, too."

"He would not like that you've turned his ranch into a farm, but he'd do it for you." Faye hugged Pepper. He saw tears in both women's eyes. His own chest tightened.

"Don't cry," his little girl said as she hugged the women's legs. Butch sat on Pepper's feet in sympathy.

He couldn't take the tears. He knew they would flow. They were women who felt deeply but their tears cut him down to the soles of his boots. "Enough of that. Gene's good in cowboy heaven and there's a potluck to judge."

"*S-e-x, s-e-x, s-e-x,*" EllaJayne sang.

He joined the women's laughter, catching the happy glint in Pepper's gaze along with the promise for later. Yep. Sex. It was a good thing.

IF PEPPER SAW another pie, she was going to throw up. The Potluck Contest had been more popular than she'd expected. Next year—if she survived tonight—they needed more judges. She thought even AJ was feeling a little queasy from all the tastings. She pulled EllaJayne tight against her where she sat listening to Danny read off the winners. She hoped by later tonight her too-full stomach wouldn't be still making her feel a little green around the gills because she had lots of plans for her cowboy. She glanced over at AJ again. He leaned back in a lawn chair, looking as comfortable there as on the back of his horse Benny who'd found his way to the ranch to live happily among the furballs. She smiled to herself. Santa Faye Ranch was more ranch-like than she'd ever imagined even with the gardens. She was content. For now.

She felt more than saw AJ sit up. What had happened? What was going on? She looked around and noticed everyone staring at them.

"AJ and Pepper, get up here," Danny said, motioning for them to approach the stage. Grammy Marie whisked EllaJayne from her arms.

"Go on," the older woman said, a huge grin splitting her face.

What was Danny up to?

AJ grasped her hand and she figured she could face anything. As they walked by smiling faces, she mouthed to him, "What's going on?" He shook his head, for once not covered by a hat. She needed to cut his hair. That warmed her from stem to stern. She liked giving him a haircut.

"Stop the lollygaggin', folks. We've got dancing to do," Danny said, giving them a mock glare.

She and AJ stepped onto the low stage with the band now set up.

"Up here to the microphone, so everyone can hear you."

AJ pushed her a little forward. He might be a big brave former bull rider but speaking in front of a crowd made him a palm-sweating mess.

"Faye," Danny said into the mic and her mother magically appeared on stage.

AJ squeezed Pepper's hand hard. With Faye involved, this could be anything. Everyone in the crowd were smiling. They were listening.

"All of you have been touched by my daughter and her cowboy. We're all here because of them. Look at this amazing event and what's planned for next year. Who would have imagined her idea for a garden to provide us all with good wholesome food would end up with a weaving circle and a soon-to-be Angel Crossing Market, where we can sell what we grow and make, no matter the weather and more than one day a week. Gene would be so proud." Faye's voice broke a little but she went on immediately. "So how do we repay that sort of commitment and kindness? The pie was great, as were all the other dishes, but we—the women of Angel Crossing—decided we needed to do more."

Oh, crap. She glanced at AJ and saw a similarly worried look on his face. She started forward to tell Faye she didn't need to do anything. Her mother went on before she could take one step.

"With the help of the ladies—"

"And the men," one of the cowboy-hatted guys who hung out at the diner piped up.

"And men. We laid out the foundation for a house of your own at Santa Faye Ranch. We've got the plan and most of the materials. It's time you and AJ and, of course, that darling EllaJayne started a home of your own. Plus my place is too small. I looked at your tea leaves, and you'll have at least five children."

Everyone cheered and laughed, while Pepper gasped in surprise. She and AJ figured they would make do with the cobbled-together, too-small ranch house until they could afford to build what they needed. She'd never imagined they'd have the money to move into a place of their own for years and years.

"Oh, my, they are speechless." Faye laughed. "We did it."

Pepper looked over the crowd of smiling faces. She saw patients. She saw people who needed her help. But what she also saw were friends, who would do this for AJ and her because they cared. It didn't matter if anyone saw her tears. This was such an amazing day. She looked at her mother, who was openly crying. She ran into her arms for a hug. "Faye. Mom. Thank you. Thank you."

"Don't thank me. Thank Angel Crossing. They love you almost as much as I do."

Pepper gathered her wits and wiped at her eyes. She went to the microphone and knew AJ was beside her without having to see him.

"Thank you," she said into the microphone. "I thought today couldn't get any better. We had this amazing potluck, and everyone had a good time. And we even had a few healthy dishes. We are so on our way. That was thanks enough for me. Honestly. This house. Well, I never expected or would have asked—" She couldn't say anymore because of the tears.

AJ stepped forward and wiped his palm on his

jeans. "When I stopped in Angel Crossing to pay my respects to my cousin, I expected to stay one night, maybe two. I was a bull rider with a baby. I had no real plan. Then I met Pepper. She took us in...even if she didn't want to." Everyone laughed. "In less than two years, I went from cowboy to farmer. You know what that's like." More laughter.

Pepper stared at her cowboy. How could she ever have imagined he was selfish and uncaring?

"What I'm trying to say is I am the one who wants to thank all of you. Without this town, we wouldn't have the ranch and we wouldn't have EllaJayne safe with us."

Pepper listened to the silence and went to the microphone, finally sure what she needed to say, "AJ is right that we owe everyone here thanks, but I've learned that allowing others to help is also a gift. So, we thank you for your help on getting our new home started. Thank you for coming out today."

Shouts echoed around the open lot.

Then Danny took over as AJ pulled her in for a hug and a kiss into the top of her hair. "You always know what to say or do. Must be why I love you."

Danny said, "Will you two lead us in our first dance?"

"Hell," AJ said. "I can't dance."

"You weren't a farmer either and look how well you've done at that."

"Guess so. Come on, honey. Let's show them how it's done."

Pepper snuggled into AJ's chest, allowing him to rock her around the dusty lot to the slow crooning of the band. She didn't care what happened next because this was all she needed.

Then a little girl voice carried over everything, singing to her own tune: "*S-e-x, s-e-x, s-e-x.*"

Everyone laughed. AJ said, "That's our girl."

* * * * *

REQUEST YOUR FREE BOOKS!
2 FREE NOVELS PLUS 2 FREE GIFTS!

♦ HARLEQUIN®

Western Romance

ROMANCE THE ALL-AMERICAN WAY!

YES! Please send me 2 FREE Harlequin® Western Romance novels and my 2 FREE gifts (gifts are worth about $10). After receiving them, if I don't wish to receive any more books, I can return the shipping statement marked "cancel." If I don't cancel, I will receive 4 brand-new novels every month and be billed just $4.74 per book in the U.S. or $5.49 per book in Canada. That's a savings of at least 12% off the cover price! It's quite a bargain! Shipping and handling is just 50¢ per book in the U.S. and 75¢ per book in Canada.* I understand that accepting the 2 free books and gifts places me under no obligation to buy anything. I can always return a shipment and cancel at any time. Even if I never buy another book, the two free books and gifts are mine to keep forever.

154/354 HDN GJ5V

Name	(PLEASE PRINT)

Address	Apt. #

City	State/Prov.	Zip/Postal Code

Signature (if under 18, a parent or guardian must sign)

Mail to the **Reader Service:**
IN U.S.A.: P.O. Box 1867, Buffalo, NY 14240-1867
IN CANADA: P.O. Box 609, Fort Erie, Ontario L2A 5X3

Want to try two free books from another line?
Call 1-800-873-8635 or visit www.ReaderService.com.

HWR16

SPECIAL EXCERPT FROM

⬡ HARLEQUIN®
™

Western Romance

*The minute he recovers from injury, Trace Delaney
will get back to bull riding, pick up and move on as
he always does. But can Annie Owen and her twin
daughters change his mind?*

Read on for a sneak preview of
THE BULL RIDER'S HOMECOMING,
the second book in Jeannie Watt's
MONTANA BULL RIDERS *miniseries.*

The girls were waiting at the top of the stairs when Annie
opened the cellar door. They high-fived their mom, and
Trace grinned as they went to stand on the heater vents
when the furnace began to blow.

"No more dollar eating," Katie announced.

"Just the normal amount of dollar eating," Annie
corrected before shooting a look Trace's way.

Dismissed?

"Well…those chores are waiting," he said.

"We can play a game next time you come by," Kristen
assured him.

Trace crouched down in front of her, feeling only a little
awkward as he said, "I look forward to that. And it was a
lot of fun riding with you guys today."

"We're not guys. We're girls," Kristen informed him.

"I stand corrected," Trace said as he got to his feet.
Tough crowd.

"I'll walk you to your truck," Annie said.

Escorted from the premises. So much for that whisper of disappointment he'd thought he saw cross her face. Maybe he was the one who was disappointed. But he'd promised to leave as soon as the furnace was fixed, and he was a man of his word.

Annie slipped into her coat and followed Trace out of the house. The air was still brisk from the storm, but the setting sun cast warm golden light over Annie's neatly kept yard. Everything about her place was warm and homey, the exact opposite of what he knew when he'd been growing up. He hoped the twins would look back in the years ahead and appreciate the home their mother had made for them.

Trace stopped before opening his truck door and looked down at Annie, who was wearing a cool expression. The woman was hard to read. On the one hand, he thought maybe she liked him. On the other, she couldn't hurry him out of there fast enough.

"Thanks again," she said.

"Anytime." One corner of his mouth quirked up before he said, "I mean that, you know."

Annie's lips compressed and she nodded, then she raised her hand and brushed her fingers against his cheek, just as he'd done to her earlier. He felt his breath catch at the light touch. Then he captured her hand with his and leaned down to take her lips in a kiss that surprised both of them.

Don't miss
THE BULL RIDER'S HOMECOMING
by Jeannie Watt, available September 2016 wherever
Harlequin® Western Romance
books and ebooks are sold.

www.Harlequin.com

Wrangle Your Friends for the Ultimate Ranch Girls' Getaway

Win an all-expenses-paid 3-night luxurious stay for you and your 3 guests at The Resort at Paws Up in Greenough, Montana.

Retail Value $10,000

A TOAST TO FRIENDSHIP, AN ADVENTURE OF A LIFETIME!

Learn more at
www.Harlequinranchgetaway.com

Sweepstakes ends August 31, 2016

WCHMR

THE WORLD IS BETTER WITH

Romance

Harlequin has everything from contemporary, passionate and heartwarming to suspenseful and inspirational stories.

Whatever your mood, we have a romance just for you!

Connect with us to find your next great read, special offers and more.

f /HarlequinBooks

🐦 @HarlequinBooks

www.HarlequinBlog.com

www.Harlequin.com/Newsletters

H HARLEQUIN

A *Romance* FOR EVERY MOOD™

www.Harlequin.com